# FOR THE SAKE OF HIS BELOVED DAUGHTER

EMMA CARTWRIGHT

This is a work of fiction. Any names or characters, businesses or places, events or incidents, are fictitious. Any resemblance to actual persons, living or dead, or actual events is purely coincidental.

**Copyright © 2024 by Emma Cartwright**
All rights reserved.

No part of this book may be reproduced in any form or by any electronic or mechanical means, including information storage and retrieval systems, without written permission from the author, except for the use of brief quotations in a book review.
**Email: emma@emmacartwrightauthor.com**

# CHAPTER 1

*A*t one o'clock, the cuckoo squawked on the hour, causing Annie to jump in her place, the needle in her hand pricking through her finger in unison. Lydia shook her head, glancing over as Annie stared at the blood in shock.

"Oh!" the young woman grumbled as her best friend swallowed a laugh, casting aside the quilt on her lap to tend to the small cut. "How does that clock always manage to startle me?"

"I don't know," Lydia replied, reaching for Annie's hand, a strand of auburn hair falling over her teal eyes as she examined the innocuous wound on the blonde woman's finger. As she suspected, it was hardly worthy of a fuss, a fact that Annie confirmed with her next words.

"It's *nix*," Annie laughed, withdrawing her hand. "Nothing I haven't done every hour before this one. I don't know how I never learn."

Giggling, the women resumed their task, gathering the quilt back over their legs to continue as Annie popped her finger into her mouth to gently suck the blood away. Even so, she continued their conversation from before it was so rudely interrupted by the wall clock.

"Will you *hilf* with Leah's *hochzich*?" Annie asked through her mouthful of finger, her bright blue eyes studying her friend's face with interest. Lydia peered up from her handiwork, her pulse quickening at the reminder of the upcoming wedding. She had not really forgotten about it, the event always in the back of her mind, like all weddings were, but she had managed to keep it in the recesses until Annie had roused the subject again.

"*Yah*, of course," Lydia replied, nodding. "I've taken on the task of *blumm*."

"*Yah*, you're the best at the flower arrangements. You have such a *gut* eye for them. I loved what you did at Sarah's," Annie gushed. She lowered her voice, removing her hand from her face to glance furtively toward the threshold of the living room before training her gaze back on Lydia again. "I hope you'll do my wedding too one day...if I can ever catch the eye of someone in particular."

She grinned sheepishly and lowered her eyes.

"I've always had a silly idea that maybe you and I would have a joint wedding one day."

Lydia's rueful grin grew, half-amused, half-saddened.

"Maybe I'll become a florist," she joked. "What with all these weddings I'm planning for other people. As far as a joint wedding goes—I think I'll be planning yours well before anyone even looks in my direction."

Annie sat back and got to work on her patches, shaking her head, the strap of her prayer bonnet falling against her cheek.

"I'm not married either," she reminded her friend. "Not for lack of trying."

Again, her eyes moved toward the hallway and Lydia snickered lightly. "You know that Daniel can't hear you, *yah*? He's out working in the fields."

Annie grimaced and flopped back against the chair, quickening her movements against the quilt. "Would it matter if he were in the *haus*?" she muttered, annoyed. "Even when he's in earshot, he doesn't seem to notice my attention. What is wrong with your *bruder*?"

Lydia maintained the serene smile on her lips, but inside, her heart sank. Immediately, Annie noticed the shift in her demeanor and again set the blanket aside. "*Wat* is it, Lydie?"

Lydia shook her head quickly, not wanting to trouble her with petty nonsense on the sunny springtime afternoon.

"It's *nix*," she reassured Annie. "We should have done this outside. Why did we coop ourselves up in here?"

"It was raining," Annie reminded her. "And we were baking bread. We didn't want to burn it, like we did last time."

Lydia giggled again, recalling the fiasco of the overdone loaves from several weeks ago.

"We could move outside now," Lydia proposed. "The *brot* is safely out of the oven and not apt to burn the *haus* down."

Annie raised an eyebrow with interest. "Your *bruder* is out there, *yah*?"

Lydia laughed lightly again. "*Yah*. But I don't know what part of the farm he's on right now."

"That's *gut* enough for me."

Lydia wagged a finger playfully. "If I didn't know better, Annie, I'd think you only came over here to make eyes at Danny."

Annie frowned, sincerely hurt by the comment.

"You will always *komme* first to me—even if your *schtupid bruder* never figures out how I feel about him."

They rose to collect their threading and patches, heading toward the front porch as Annie strained to look for signs of Daniel Yoder while Lydia settled into one of the rocking chairs on the veranda.

The blonde woman looked about hopefully, but her excitement was instantly dashed as she realized that Daniel wasn't in view.

"Of course, he's nowhere in sight," Annie grumbled. "That's just my luck, isn't it?"

"It's not as if you don't see him every day." Lydia laughed. "Stay for *nachtesse*. You'll see him then."

"Not that it will make any difference," Annie moaned again, plopping herself in the neighboring rocking chair to collect her side of the quilt onto her lap. "What is wrong with that *bu*? Doesn't he see me?"

"He can't help but see you, Annie. You're beautiful and always here."

"Maybe he just sees me as a *schweschder* then," she moaned. Lydia shrugged, unsure of how her brother envisioned her best friend. Lydia had never broached the subject, hardly having any knowledge of relationships herself.

Annie paled. "Is he seeing someone else?"

She stared intently at her best friend. "You would tell me, wouldn't you, Lydie?"

"*Yah*, of course," Lydia said, and laughed. "He's just *schtupid*. Maybe he doesn't realize you're interested. You could just tell him, you know."

Annie groaned loudly. "I don't know how to be any clearer! And I don't want to embarrass him, or myself. It's his job to approach me if he has any interest. Maybe it's time for me to set my sights on someone else. *Wat* do you think?"

Lydia balked.

"I think you're asking the wrong *frau* for advice on *mannsleit*," she told Annie bluntly. "Even if it is about my *bruder*."

Embarrassment colored Annie's face and she bit on her lower lip, the quest for Daniel's attention suddenly losing speed as she eyed Lydia with deep sympathy. Instantly, Lydia wished she had not said anything, heat tinging her cheeks.

"You'll find a *gut mann*," Annie promised with her usual optimism. "How could you not?"

Avoiding her eyes, Lydia fixated on the task in her hands, the question weighing heavier on her than she cared to admit. It was one that she had asked herself too many times over the years. She had watched her friends pair off and marry while she had not been approached with any interest even once.

"You just need to be patient," Annie went on, warming to her usual spiel of confidence. "I should probably take my own advice, too. It doesn't help that I'm constantly complaining about Danny, I'm sure."

"I'm afraid that I'm running out of time for patience," Lydia replied with a sigh. "I'm not getting any younger, Annie."

"But you *are* getting smarter," Annie replied, rolling her eyes. "And these foolish *mannsleit* can't handle it. I suspect that's most of the problem."

Lydia blushed fully now, gnawing on the insides of her cheeks. "I'm not that smart," she muttered.

"Oh no?" Annie laughed. "You do nothing but read all the time. You know more than the Bishop. It's no wonder that all the men in the community are terrified of you. They don't deserve you, either."

Exhaling, Lydia stared at her friend. It was not the compliment that Annie had intended. "This doesn't *hilf* my position. I want to be married and start a *familye*. My poor *vadder* is worried about me."

"Maybe you need to…branch out," Annie suggested, waving her hands around.

Lydia raised an eyebrow. "Branch out?" she repeated.

"*Yah*. Everyone in Calico knows who you are. The single *mannsleit* are probably going to keep their distance because they know you're smarter than them—"

"I wish you would stop saying that," Lydia groaned. "It's not true. I'm not smarter. I just like to read. That doesn't mean I know more."

"Which intimidates them. They assume you are smarter and what *mann* wants to be with a *frau* who knows more than him?" Annie said. She hesitated. "Have you thought about putting the books down when the men are around? You could always keep your reading to yourself."

Lydia had considered doing that many times. It had been suggested to her in the past, but she wondered if she truly wanted to draw in a husband under false pretenses. Eventually, she would return to devouring her texts, burying her face in the words in which she found more comfort than she did the world. It was her escape and her way of learning. It was not fair to ask her to give up something she loved.

"I won't hide who I am," she told Annie softly, and her friend appeared contrite at the suggestion. "*Gott* made me as I am, and He would not want me to hide my true self or else He would not have made me this way."

Annie bobbed her head in agreement.

"*Nee*, and you shouldn't. You are beautiful and smart and hard working. Any *mann* would be blessed to court you. I'm sorry I suggested it."

"We just need to convince the *mannsleit* of that," Lydia quipped lightly.

Annie gave her another look filled with compassion. "I'm not married either," she told Lydia firmly. "Maybe it's just the *mannsleit* of Lancaster county. There's obviously a problem here."

Lydia laughed as Annie grinned encouragingly. "Clearly there is something wrong with them all—particularly your *bruder*. There must be something in the *wasser*. The only *gut mannsleit* are our *vadders*."

Lydia returned her smile, but inside, her heart remained low in her chest. She was grateful for Annie's chirping support and friendship, but she did not look forward to another season of weddings and courtships, which had nothing to do with her.

*Maybe she's right. Maybe I should give up on all the reading and focus only on finding a mann. Time is running out for me and soon there won't be any eligible men left in the county for me.*

That did not seem like a good motivator to change her entire personality. But living at home with her father forever was not the future that Lydia wanted, either.

"*Hallo*, Annie."

Lydia's reverie was shaken as her father approached the front of the house as if on cue to her thoughts, his hands full of firewood for inside.

"*Hallo*, Simeon," Annie called back sweetly. "Your cuckoo clock scared me again today."

Simeon Yoder laughed heartily, shaking his graying head. "How many years have you been *cooma* to our *haus*, Annie, and you still haven't grown accustomed to that bird?"

"I think she likes the thrill of it, *Daed*," Lydia joked and Simeon snickered again, making his way toward the front door.

"I get so few thrills otherwise," Annie remarked dryly.

"You two," Simeon sighed.

"Is Danny *cooma* soon?" Annie called out hopefully to Simeon's retreating back. Lydia swallowed a groan at her friend's shameless question.

Simeon cast her a quick glance over his shoulder. "He's gone to town today," he answered. "He's not here."

The screen door slammed in his wake and Annie moaned dramatically. "That really is just my luck, isn't it?"

Lydia shook her head in wonderment.

"*Wat?*" Annie asked, catching her expression. "I had hoped to see him today."

"*Nix. Komme*, let's get this done," she urged, raising the quilt. "I have to get *nachtesse* started."

Annie leaned closer, her blue eyes twinkling mischievously. "Would it bother you if I became your true *schweschder* after I married your *bruder?*" she teased, as she had so many times before. But today, it struck Lydia in a different way and her sadness hit full peak now. Annie's grin faded away as she realized her jesting was hitting a sour note for her friend. Her brow knitted into a vee.

"Lydie, what is it? I'm only playing with you. Your *bruder* doesn't even know I'm alive but as your *freind*. You don't have to worry about us...I don't think. Is that what's bothering you?"

Lydia shook her head vehemently.

"*Nee*, it's not you," she said truthfully. "I..."

"*Wat* then? Tell me." Annie set the quilt aside and reached for Lydia's hand, concern coloring her face. "Whatever it is, you can tell me. I didn't mean to upset you."

"You didn't—not really. It's not you...not you specifically."

Annie studied her face, attempting to keep her own impassive, and Lydia struggled to put her feelings into words.

"I envy your confidence. If you don't find happiness with Daniel, you'll find it with someone else," Lydia rushed out, months of pent-up emotions flowing from her mouth in a torrent. "I will never find it with anyone. No one has ever shown me any interest."

"Oh, Lydia, you will find it—" Annie sputtered, her face paling as she recognized the true anguish in her friend's expression.

"*Nee*, I don't think I will," Lydia interjected, dropping her head. "And I think I'm *cooma* to accept that now. But it's hard, what with all these weddings and talk of *lieb* and courtships flowing around me. I think spring is always the hardest time of year for me for that reason."

"Oh…"

Guilt covered Annie's face, but she tipped Lydia's face upward, firmness overtaking her eyes. "*Nee*. I refuse to believe that someone as *wunderbar* as you will not find a *gut mann* of your own, Lydie. How could *Gott* want that for you? It would be such a waste."

She shook her head so hard it was a wonder her bonnet did not fly off her blonde head.

"We will ask Him, *yah*?"

"Ask who?" Lydia stared at Annie in confusion.

"*Gott. Gott* has a plan, and we must ask Him what it is for you. Pray with me."

She bowed her head as Lydia stared at her skeptically. "Right now?"

"*Yah*, right now. Isn't this when you need guidance?" Annie demanded. "When else are you going to ask Him? We pray to *Gott* when we need Him and we need Him now, don't we?"

"Oh, Annie—"

"Don't 'Oh Annie' me. We must focus on what we need from *Gott* and He will provide, just like He always does," Annie intoned, her confidence inspiring Lydia as always. It was difficult to say no to Annie when she was always so full of hope.

*I may not have a husband or kinner, but I do have a very gut friend in Annie. I am blessed in other ways. I should count those blessings instead of bemoaning what I don't have. I would be blessed to have her as my schweschder. I do hope Danny eventually comes to his senses about her.*

Annie pulled on her hand and nodded for Lydia to bow her head. Together, they closed their eyes quietly.

*Dear Gott, don't let me die an ault maed in my vadder's haus, alone and childless. Please let me find someone who doesn't think I'm too bookish and boring.*

After a moment of silence, the women raised their heads and Annie stared expectantly at Lydia.

"Do you feel better?" she asked hopefully. Lydia smiled warmly at her friend and nodded honestly.

"*Yah*," she answered, ignoring the lingering ache in her heart. "I do. *Denki*, Annie."

Relief painted her face and Annie reclaimed her seat. "*Gut*. Now let's back to *warrick* before this *mann* wanders in to sweep you off your feet and I have to schedule in your time."

Lydia's grin was genuine now as she envisioned such an improbable event, but it was still nice to imagine.

# CHAPTER 2

An upbeat pop song played quietly on the back speakers of the car, snatches of the music catching the edges of Jacob's ears but lost before he could properly identify what it was exactly. Not that he was trying too intently. He wasn't in a dancing to the music kind of mood.

His eyes burned from the driving, the pinks and blues of twilight threatening to overwhelm the backroads on which he drove. A dull throbbing emanated between his eyes, and he used his right thumb to massage it away.

Reaching for his stale coffee, he took a swig, the liquid almost spraying from his lips as a shriek radiated from behind him.

"MOO!" came the delighted cry from the back, causing Jacob to jump, his frayed nerves snapping despite the fact that this was at least the twelfth time the call had come. "MOO!"

Barely managing to swallow, Jacob steeled himself, setting the cold, disgusting drink back in the stained holder in the console.

"MOO, Daddy!"

He half glanced over his shoulder and offered his daughter a taut smile.

"Yes, Amy. Look at the cows," he intoned again. He was sure that sentence was going to rule his nightmares that night. "There are lots of cows around here, aren't there, peanut?"

"The cow goes moo!" Amy chirped.

"Yes, it does," Jacob mumbled, turning his tired eyes back toward the road. Twisting his stiff neck, he readjusted his hands on the steering wheel.

The last of the springtime sunshine slid under the horizon and a blanket of blue encompassed the countryside. The GPS glitched slightly and Jacob grimaced. "Don't fail on me now," he muttered.

"What, Daddy?"

"Pardon, Amy. Say 'pardon,'" he mumbled by rote.

"Daddy, bawk!" she said instead. He didn't acknowledge Amy this time, but his twenty-two-month-old daughter was not one to be ignored and raised her voice to ensure that she was heard. "DADDY! CHICKS! BAWK! BAWK! BAWK!"

"I see them," he fibbed through clenched teeth, glancing at his cell phone on the mounted charger. The GPS kicked back in and he exhaled with relief.

*We're not that far out of the way of civilization. We're still close enough to everything. This is a good, safe place. Safe being the most important thing.*

"Daddy, chickens!" Amy yelled again. "YOU SEE CHICKIES?!"

Jacob inhaled a shaky breath.

"It's getting late, peanut," he told her soothingly.

"BAWK! BAWK! BAWK!" she howled, ignoring his subtle hint. Subtly was not for toddlers.

"Amy, close your eyes," he told her, trying desperately to keep the aggravation from his voice. It wasn't the child he was upset with after all. It was never about Amy and her endless questions. It had just been a harrowing few days, the packing and driving and ultimate decision-making wearing him down to reserve proportions. The covertness of the move and the planning had only further eaten at his wits.

Now, the home stretch was proving to be his breaking point.

"Not tired," Amy replied in a singsong voice. "Old Macdonald had a farm, E-I-E-I-O!"

*Oh God. Not now. Please. Not nursery rhymes.*

"Amy," he interjected placatingly. "We're almost at the hotel. Why don't you have some of your Goldfish crackers and then we'll find a Cracker Barrel for dinner."

Abruptly, the girl stopped her crooning, her huge, gray eyes lighting up in the rear-view as her blonde curls cocked against the car seat. "Chicken fingies?"

"Yep. Chicken fingies and fries and ketchup," Jacob promised. "But you have to just stay quiet for a few more miles, okay, honey? Can you do that for me?"

She studied him pensively, and Jacob's heart exploded in pain.

*God, she looks exactly like Nancy when she does that. She looks more and more like Nancy every day.*

"Okay, Daddy."

"Thank you, peanut."

He watched as she dug out her own snacks, shoveling a small handful in her mouth before sticking her sippy cup between her lips and in less than five minutes, her eyes hooded as she lulled herself off to sleep. But the pain lingered in Jacob's heart as darkness encompassed the minivan. Suddenly, he wished she were awake and squeaking at him, reminding him of her mother. The hollow pit of pain burrowed deeper somehow and with it came the daunting realization.

*I'll never outrun it,* he thought, his strong hands gripping the steering wheel tighter, his knuckles turning white with the gesture. *It won't matter where I go. I'll never outrun the pain of losing Nancy. I could take Amy to Tibet and it will still be just as strong and hurt as much.*

A logical side of him had always known that. This move to Calico, where his grandfather had once lived in the Amish community before abandoning it for the outside world, had not come lightly. But after a year of living in Philadelphia in the wake of Nancy's violent end, it was impossible to ignore the amount of human suffering and crime that existed around them. Coupled with the living hell that Nancy's family had made his life, Jacob had been left with few choices in the aftermath.

He lived every day in constant fear that something would happen to Amy now, every set of eyes a threat in the most basic of circumstances. Even after quitting his job, he never felt as if he could let his daughter out of his sight, the doors were never locked tightly enough. His protectiveness brimmed paranoia and Jacob knew that drastic changes needed to be made.

Nancy would not have wanted their child raised like that, not when Amy had already come so close to losing her life in the same gang violence that had claimed his wife's life. Jacob's mounting disillusionment in the city didn't help matters. It hadn't been a healthy situation for anyone, regardless of how hard Nancy's family had fought for him to stay. Their behavior had only made things worse.

A simple blue sign appeared on the right, announcing their arrival in Calico suddenly, and a sense of peace overcame Jacob. The sensation was shocking, and again his sensibilities told him it was a placebo, but all the same, he felt as if he could breathe for the first time in over a year. It wasn't strong enough to overtake his grief or guilt, but it offered him some semblance of security.

*No one is going to get caught up in a drive-by on the highway here,* he thought grimly. *Amy isn't going to get kidnapped or shot.*

But as he drove past the signage, more doubts began to plague him, different doubts.

*Am I really doing this? Can I really do this? Should I really do this?*

Back in the city, it had seemed like a great idea, whisking his daughter away to seclusion and attempting to reclaim a legacy that technically wasn't lost to him. His grandfather had never been baptized and, therefore, had not been banished from the community. There were still family members of his in the Amish district—according to Oscar. The stories his grandfather had told him as a boy had always made Jacob feel a sense of enchanted connection to the Amish, and when he'd had the opportunity, he had investigated his history.

Jacob had made day trips to Calico in his youth with his parents, but nothing more than a trip to the farmer's markets. But for his grandfather's loving mentions of the rural country in which he had been raised, Jacob knew very little about the ways of the community. He only knew that his grandfather missed it terribly and often wished that he had not left.

"Not that I didn't love your grandmother," Oscar had added quickly when Jacob stared at him accusingly. "She was the reason I left in the first place, and I wouldn't have traded my family for anything. But I often wondered what life would have been like if I'd brought her back with me instead of the other way around."

"You could have done that?" Jacob had asked as a boy, amazed to learn that the Amish would allow an outsider to join them. "You could have brought Gramma back to live with you?"

"It would have been difficult," Oscar replied. "But if your grandmother was willing to put in the effort, it could have been done."

Jacob had never really learned what was involved with such a conversion until he was interested in it himself and he considered the uphill battle in front of him.

*I can't think like that,* he scolded himself, steering the vehicle off the main road toward a side street where the electronic map guided him. *I will do whatever is required for Amy's sake. I don't care how hard it is.*

But as the half-burned neon lights of the single-storey motel appeared ahead, another wave of apprehension washed through Jacob. He had quit his job—unapologetically. He didn't miss it, nor did he want to return to it. But those skills were the only ones he had, starting directly out of college. They were not skills that would not be well revered in a pacifistic community like this one.

More uneasiness swelled inside him. Swallowing, he pulled into the lot and peered back at his still-sleeping daughter, his heart pounding. He debated turning around and going home, but to what? The house was gone, their furniture too. Nancy's family was by no means an option to contact, and Oscar was in a nursing home.

*My savings are non-existent. I need to find a job. That's the first order of business.*

Inhaling, he turned off the car and unbuckled his seatbelt, cringing at the thought of waking up Amy. But he couldn't leave her in the car…could he?

Suddenly, he looked around at the desolate area, the realization that he wasn't in Philadelphia anymore hitting him like a happy punch. Still, he didn't risk it and slowly removed his slumbering toddler from her car seat.

"Chicken fingies?" Amy mumbled.

"Not yet, peanut," Jacob told her. "We're going to get a room first, okay?"

"Moo!" she mumbled back, draping her arms over his shoulder, her soft breath nuzzling into his neck. Jacob wrapped his arms tightly around her and made his way into the office, bouncing her gently in his embrace until a bleary-eyed woman emerged from the back. She blinked in surprise to see the man with the baby.

"Aww, isn't she precious!" the clerk murmured softly, peering at Amy. "How old?"

"Twenty-two-months," Jacob mumbled. "Can we get a room?"

The clerk looked at Amy. "Does she need a crib? I don't have one."

"No…two twin beds will work."

The woman's face twisted into an indiscernible expression. "You and the missus are going to share a twin?"

"It's just me and Amy," Jacob muttered tersely, not liking all the questions. A fusion of conflict and concern crossed over her face, and Jacob pursed his lips.

*I must look like some weirdo to her.*

He debated explaining his situation, but he didn't want to air out his personal story to this stranger.

"How many nights?" she asked, her tone oddly flat. Jacob knew she was trying to read him.

*She's trying to figure out whether or not to call the cops on me,* he thought ruefully. *Oh, the irony.*

Jacob shifted his weight uncomfortably and bit on his lower lip, darting his eyes away. "I'm not sure," he admitted. "We're new in town and trying to get set up."

The woman nodded, scribbling down something he couldn't see on a piece of paper. "That's no problem, honey. It's slow for the next few weeks anyway, but we might need to renegotiate then."

She was still studying him through her peripheral vision, but he could tell she was relaxing on her opinion.

Jacob swallowed, afraid to ask the cost. "Can I just give you my credit card? You can charge it for incidentals?"

"Uh, huh?" He wiggled his wallet out of his back pocket, balancing Amy in his arms, and she watched him speculatively. "Where you from?"

"Philly."

"Hm." Accepting the card, she only took the number and Jacob realized she didn't even have a machine to run it through.

*Is that good or bad? Am I about to be defrauded or helped? Am I in Twin Peaks?*

He was too exhausted to worry about it.

"Room 115—just to your left, honey."

"Thanks." He reached for the key and paused, turning in embarrassment. Clearing his throat, he added, "Do you happen to know if anyone is hiring? I don't really care what kind of job."

Sympathy sprang into her eyes as if she were truly seeing the father for the first time, and she shook her head slowly.

"Like I said, Mr. Troyer, it's low season, so this isn't really hiring time…"

Jacob nodded and turned away. "Thanks."

"Troyer…is that an Amish name?" she called out.

He paused and looked back at her. "I…well, kind of…yes."

She pursed her lips thoughtfully. "You could always try the district. The farms are always looking for extra hands. They don't necessarily advertise in town, but if you try your luck going door to door. Of course, with the little one…"

She shrugged. "But they do like to procreate, so they might not be opposed to your little one hanging around. They might even have a few little ones to keep her entertained. But like I said before, I'm just spit balling here."

Jacob stared at her, his pulse quickening.

*This has to be a sign from God right here. I came here to get a leg into the Amish community and my first lead is into the Amish community.*

He nodded vigorously, a grin growing over his face. "Yes! Thank you...?" he stared at her, embarrassed to realize he hadn't learned her name.

"Mara... Thompson."

He exhaled, and they shared another smile.

"Mara. Thank you so much!"

"Don't thank me yet. They can be very close-knit and difficult to approach," she warned. Disappointment touched Jacob's soul at the revelation.

"I-I had heard they were very kind."

Mara nodded. "They are very hospitable and warm, but that is different than allowing you into their fold. I'm only warning you so that you don't get your hopes up. I don't know why you would have come to Calico, of all places, looking for work. The market isn't exactly booming in these parts. You'd be better off going to Wilmington or Allentown. Definitely better opportunities out those ways."

Jacob grinned. "I have family in these parts," he replied evasively, not wanting to get into the details. He wasn't sure how his presence might be received, and he didn't want his arrival to blindside anyone before he could properly approach the appropriate people.

*Whoever they are. I really should have picked Grandpa's brain more on the matter before I came out here.*

He vowed to call on Oscar the next day.

"But I appreciate all your advice," Jacob added quickly. "It's duly noted."

She returned his smile and turned away. "Let me know if you need anything else, Mr. Troyer."

"Call me Jake. All my friends do."

*Not that I have many of those anymore.*

"All right, Jake. Good night."

For the first time since packing up his house and belongings and putting Amy in the car for Lancaster County, Jacob felt a wave of true hope as if God had finally heard his prayer for guidance and answered him.

*It probably didn't help that I turned my back on You,* Jacob thought, swallowing yet another torrent of shame that threatened to encompass him. This bout of guilt would have to take a number. Between the survivor's guilt and constant surety that every decision he made was wrong, the regret he had for abandoning God was low on his list.

But if he hoped to curry any favor among his grandfather's people and regain his place among them in a place he was sure his daughter would be safe forever, he would need to make sure God was good with him, too.

If God were on his side, maybe he could convince the district elders that an ex-cop from Philadelphia was worthy of conversion to their community.

# CHAPTER 3

Sandrine, the oldest and surliest of Simeon's hens, was particularly finicky that morning as Lydia tried to feed and collect from the flock. She squawked and fussed, forbidding Lydia to enter the roost, keeping the young woman outside with her feed in hand, bargaining with a chicken.

"*Komme* now, Sandrine," she begged the fowl. "What's gotten into you today?"

Belligerently, the hen squeaked again and flapped her wings, a flurry of feathers flying everywhere in response. Her agitation only riled the others and suddenly, Lydia was encased by a bunch of annoyed chickens.

"Goodness," she grumbled, trying again to push inside, but once more, her plans were foiled as Sandrine pecked at her. "Would you rather starve today?"

A little giggle whirled Lydia around, the foreign sound of a child's laughter nearby startling her. For a moment, she thought she was dreaming when she saw the blonde cherub against the gate, her chubby hands extended toward one of the wayward hens, a tall, stately stranger behind her.

"No, Amy, don't touch them," the man chided her softly.

"It's all right," Lydia choked, realizing she was not having some kind of divine reverie after all. "They won't hurt her."

The man straightened himself as she ventured away from the coop, his verdant eyes locking on hers. A hot flush crept down Lydia's neck, the handsomeness of his face drawing her closer.

*He's an Englischer,* she thought with deep disappointment. The realization almost made her laugh. *As if that makes any difference to you.*

Cautiously, but with a smile, Lydia approached, her head cocked curiously. "Are you lost?" she asked kindly, her eyes trailing toward the nearby van parked at the road. "Town isn't very far from here."

The child again reached for the chickens, her laughter rising as one pecked harmlessly at her, engaging in play. "Chickies!"

"Be gentle now, Amy," the man told her warningly before addressing Lydia's question. The young woman hardly knew where to set her eyes, an endearment toward the child growing as she tried to pet the chickens. Simultaneously, she could not get enough of the man's angular jawline and serious, green eyes.

He had a somber look about him, a shadow hovering over his dark mane of hair, as if followed by a foreboding cloud.

"I don't think we're lost. Is this the Yoder farm?"

Lydia's heart skipped.

*He's looking for us. Who is this mann?*

He had come with his child, which discounted the idea that he had come with some kind of mal intent. Certainly, a man from the bank did not arrive in a pair of faded blue jeans and toddler on hand.

"*Yah*, it is. I'm Lydia Yoder," she replied slowly. "Who are you?"

He offered her a tired smile that did not quite light up his eyes, although she was certain she read an element of interest there.

"Forgive the intrusion," he said. "My name is Jacob Troyer. This is my daughter, Amy."

Lydia's head jerked up at the familiar surname, her eyes widening, but she could plainly see that the man was not from the district.

"We've just arrived in Calico and after visiting some of the neighboring farms, I was told that Simeon Yoder might be in need of some extra help for the spring and summer on his farm?"

Lydia's mouth slacked in shock at the brazen ask. Once in a while, a young English drifter would wander through looking for work, but never a man with his daughter. She gaped at him, unsure of what to say.

"Could I speak with your father?" he pressed, reading the stunned expression clearly. "I-I realize that I'm probably not the average guy who comes looking."

Lydia nodded, swallowing to find her voice.

"*Yah*—yes," she sputtered. "*Komme* to the *haus*—the house. I'll find him for you."

Relief fell over Jacob's face, and he reached down to pick up his daughter, who squeaked indignantly.

"No! Chickens!" she protested.

"There are horses and cows up this way," Lydia informed the child, watching her entire demeanor shift. "Would you like to see them?"

"Yey!"

"Yes, please, Amy," Jacob coached, shooting Lydia an apologetic look.

"Yes, please," Amy repeated dutifully. Lydia smiled and led the way back toward the house, casting the father and daughter another glance as she moved.

"MOO MOO, cows go moo!" Amy sang loudly.

"Shh, Amy," Jacob told her worriedly.

"There's no need to quiet her," Lydia reassured him with a chuckle. "This is a farm. Animals are always making noise."

As promised, the animals appeared as they turned around the side of the house and Amy screeched with delight, kicking to be released from her father's arms.

"No, just stay—" he started to say, but Lydia shook her head.

"She can go and see them. They're penned. They can't hurt her."

Slowly, he released her, warily eying the woman, and she nodded confidently. "I'm going to look for my *vadder*..."

She trailed off as her father suddenly appeared on the field, his gait quick. Apparently, he had heard the child's yells from where he was working.

"Never mind," Lydia murmured. "Here's my *vadder* now."

Simeon hurried toward them, his brow creased, more worry overtaking him as he saw the stranger with his daughter. "Lydie, what is this?" he asked nervously.

"*Daed*, this is Jacob Troyer," she explained before he could speak. "He's looking for *warrick*."

Simeon's face was identical to his daughters when she had first heard Jacob's plea, but the Englischer took the conversation from there.

"I know this is unorthodox, sir," he said. "But my grandfather —he was a part of this community."

Both Lydia and Simeon recoiled in disbelief.

"I don't think he was in this district, though," Jacob went on. "At least, not from what I've discovered since I've been here."

"I-I don't understand," Simeon said suspiciously, his eyes narrowing. "You're not Amish."

"No," Jacob agreed. "My grandfather left here during his Rumspringa before he was baptized. But he always spoke so fondly of his home here and the stories he told about community and faith… I had always hoped to introduce my daughter to it when she was old enough."

Lydia's eyed traveled toward little Amy, who toddled around the horse pen, the smile on her face evident even from where they stood.

"How old is she?" Lydia heard herself ask.

"She'll be two in September."

"I need permanent help, Jacob—" Simeon started to say.

"Jake, please," he interjected, his eyes lingering on Lydia. She blushed and looked away under his scrutiny, turning to busy herself with the fence line, which needed no work.

"Jake," Simeon grumbled, unmoved. "I need full-time, long-term help, not some tourist passing through."

"*Daed*," Lydia scolded her father softly.

"I'm being honest with him," Simeon insisted. "This is not a good fit for a silly vacation."

Through her peripheral vision, Lydia saw Jacob's eyes widen, surprise overtaking him. "Oh…I wasn't explaining myself properly," he mumbled, sounding embarrassed. "This…I'm not here on vacation. We're in Calico to stay."

Lydia was sure her heart would burst through her chest and she had to turn away. Her father was much less impressed.

"Where are you staying?" he demanded.

"At the Calico Roadside Motel on Spenser Avenue."

Father and daughter shared a look, but Lydia again busied herself as the men talked.

"You don't have a *haus*? A proper place for your *dochder*?" he asked dubiously. Lydia swallowed, sensing that Jacob was losing favor with her father with each word he spoke.

Jacob released a huge sigh, lowering his head as he rubbed his thumb and forefinger on the bridge of his nose.

"Can I be frank with you?" he asked, in a low voice, as if he would rather not.

"Please," Simeon insisted.

"My wife passed away just over a year ago. Her death was… sudden and…"

He stopped to collect himself, his eyes partially closing as if he might break down. "Her passing made me reconsider what was important in my life…and the relationship that I had with God—or rather, that I didn't have."

He took another breath. "More and more, I thought about what my grandfather had told me about Calico, about growing up in the Amish community, and I felt as if I were being called back here, that this was the safest place for Amy and for me. I don't just want to live in Calico. I am hoping to be integrated back into the community."

Lydia gasped aloud as Simeon's mouth dropped fully open.

"*Wat*?!" they chorused in unison.

"I know it's a huge thing," Jacob rushed on, holding up his hands. "And it's not something I'm taking lightly, but for the sake of my daughter, I'm willing to do whatever it takes. She deserves to live in a world devoid of violence and…"

Again, his voice cracked, and Lydia wanted to rush over and put her arms around him, but she did not dare.

"I-I was not expecting any of that," Simeon admitted slowly. "But I do understand the desire to do what you can for you *kinner*."

He cast Lydia a sidelong look, and she blushed, biting on her lip and unsure of what to do with her eyes now.

"I can't begrudge a *mann* for wanting to do better for his *kinner*," Simeon went on. "And I do need the *hilf*."

Jacob's face lit up in unison as he, too, realized.

"Oh, thank you, sir—"

"There's no sir nonsense here. My name is Simeon. This is Lydia."

Jacob smiled warmly, his gaze lingering on Lydia once more. "We've met."

Lydia's breath caught in her throat as she understood what her father was saying. "You will start early and the *warrick* is hard." He looked at Lydia warily. "Will you watch the *kinner*? I assume he doesn't have accommodations for her."

"It would be my pleasure," Lydia gushed, unable to keep the grin from her face. Simeon gave her a long, inscrutable look, but he finally turned back to Jacob.

"You may find that this is not for you," he went on.

"I am willing to see that for myself, but I don't think that's true, si...uh, Simeon. I believe that God called me out here for a reason. He wants me to know my roots and learn them again."

Simeon shrugged. "I suppose we'll see."

"*Daed*, can we introduce him to Bishop Kauffman?" Lydia blurted out. Both men looked at her, Jacob with interest, Simeon more cautiously.

"Maybe later, Lydie," Simeon said quietly. "It was *gut* to meet you, Jake. We will see you on Tuesday *mariye*—in the morning, *yah*?"

"*Yah*," Jacob agreed, grinning. "Thank you. Uh...*denki*."

His smile broadened as Lydia smiled approvingly and he moved off to collect his daughter, who was still trying to catch the attention of all the animals.

"Lydie, you can't get his hopes up," Simeon said with a frown the moment he was out of earshot. She turned to her father in confusion. "What do you mean?" she asked. "I'm not. He knows there is a long road ahead for him if this is what he wants."

Simeon exhaled deeply. "His story is very sad, but the fact that his *Grossdaddi* was Amish does not enable him to become part of the community. He doesn't even speak the language!"

"He can learn," Lydia replied, unfazed by her father's pessimism. "If he wants it enough, he will do it—for the sake of his *dochder*."

Jacob and Amy returned toward them, and Lydia smiled, waving them toward the road. "I'll see you off," she offered. Jacob nodded gratefully, thanking Simeon again.

"He doesn't like me, does he?" Jacob asked when they were out of her father's view. Lydia chuckled. "He wouldn't have offered you a job if not," she reassured him. "He's just worried that you might not understand what's involved when it comes to living among us."

Jacob paused and peered at her as Amy again wandered off to chase the animals. He pursed his lips together thoughtfully.

"Do you know what's involved?"

The question took her aback.

"I-I haven't known anyone to convert," she admitted. "But I imagine that you would need to know the language at a minimum."

He grimaced, gnawing on the insides of his cheeks. "Fluently?"

Lydia shrugged. "Probably?"

"Maybe he's right," he agreed. "But that doesn't matter. I'm not going back to the city. Not ever."

The determination in his tone fully convinced her. She hoped that the rest of the community would be as swayed as she was.

*Just wait until Annie sees Jacob. Our prayers really did work!*

# CHAPTER 4

"Daddy, I'm hungry," Amy announced when they returned to the minivan.

"I bet you are," Jacob agreed. "You've been so patient all morning, peanut. Let's find you something to eat, okay?"

"No chicken fingies. I no wanna eat the chickies."

Surprised but amused, Jacob agreed. "What about pizza?" he suggested instead. "I think there's a little place near the motel I saw, and we can save some for dinner, too."

Amy nodded eagerly and Jacob put the vehicle in gear, his gaze fixed on the rear-view. But this time, he wasn't looking at his daughter. The beautiful Amish woman stood in his line of vision, watching him drive away and maintaining his racing heart rate, long after he steered the vehicle away from the Yoder farm and toward Calico.

"She was nice lady," Amy sang, snapping Jacob back into the car.

"Hmm?"

"The lady with the funny hat," Amy said.

Jacob glanced at his daughter reprovingly. "That's called a prayer bonnet," he told her sternly. "It's not a funny hat. It's a sign of faith and her devotion to God."

Amy blinked at him uncomprehendingly, and Jacob sighed. They had a lot of catching up to do.

The attraction he had felt toward Lydia Yoder had shocked him. Yes, she was pretty, but that wasn't what he was feeling when he looked at her. There was compassion and intelligence in her eyes that pierced his soul, a kindness that he had rarely seen anywhere else. The combination of all her attributes made his head spin dauntingly.

*Nancy is barely cold in her grave and you're trying to start a new life here for Amy. This is not the time to be thinking about Lydia Yoder or anyone else,* he growled at himself. But as he drove, he couldn't get Lydia out of his mind, especially when Amy would not stop rousing her and the farm in conversation.

"Daddy, will we go back there? Can I see the horsies?"

"We're going back the day after tomorrow… in the *mariye*." He tried the foreign word on his lips.

*Might as well start using the language if I'm serious about this.*

Amy didn't notice, but Jacob felt foolish suddenly.

*Am I a fraud?*

He thought of how quickly Simeon Yoder had shot down the idea of Jacob meeting with the Bishop. The farmer didn't think that Jacob was ready to commit to their ways and the former cop could hardly blame him. Aside from his words, what else had he really done to show it?

It was time to really roll up his sleeves and get serious.

~

Amy fell asleep soon after they ate, but sunlight still lingered over the horizon, slipping slowly over the Pennsylvania landscape as Jacob pored over the books he had picked up after the pizza.

He rubbed his bleary eyes but refused to stop reading. He couldn't be sure that everything he was taking in was necessary to his conversion, but he wanted to consume everything in sight, lest it was pertinent.

A gentle rap at the motel room door made him jump, and he glanced at the time on the alarm clock on the nightstand. Frowning, he rose to answer it. Mara stood on the other side of the threshold, her face twisted in a peculiar knot of interest.

"I'm sorry to disturb you so late," she said. "Is the baby asleep?"

Jacob looked back at Amy, who remained unbothered by the disruption, before turning his attention back to the clerk. "Yes."

"There's a message for you at the front desk from a Gideon Kauffman." Mara thrust a piece of paper toward him. Jacob accepted the note, frowning.

"Who?" he mumbled, more to himself than Mara. The woman shrugged and turned away as Jacob scanned the note. Blinking, a grin formed on his lips.

"Did you meet this guy yourself?" he called after her. Mara paused and shook her head.

"No. Carl took the message but said he was an Amish guy."

Jacob's smile broadened. He wasn't "an Amish guy." He was "the" Amish guy.

"Thank you, Mara. Hey…I found work today. Thanks for the advice."

Her eyes brightened, and she nodded approvingly. "I'm glad to hear it—although I'm not surprised, Jake. You seem like a man who gets what he's after."

Jacob accepted the compliment with pride, bidding Mara goodnight and closing the door, the message still firmly in his hand.

He reread the neat, even scrawl.

*I understand you have requested a meeting with the elders of the district. I am Bishop Gideon Kauffman and can make time for you tomorrow at three o'clock.*

An address followed, and Jacob's heart thumped wildly in anticipation.

*Lydia must have done this for me. Her father didn't seem keen on introducing me to the elders, but she must have gone and set it up.*

Jacob could not help but think of the lovely, auburn-haired woman now as he returned to his books, the smile melded into his face.

He vowed not to disappoint her at the meeting the following day.

∼

"More chickies?" Amy inquired as they drove toward the address the Bishop had given the following afternoon.

"Uh…I'm not sure, peanut. Probably," Jacob laughed, amused by her infatuation with all things living. Farm life would not be much of an adjustment for Amy, it seemed, and for that, Jacob was grateful. It was only one of his litanies of worries, after all, but Amy was so young, she would likely not remember living in the city once they were accepted to the district.

*If we're accepted into the district.*

"Chickies," Amy insisted. "Moo cows."

"I'll see what I can do," Jacob promised, steering the minivan up a long, well-kept driveway toward a pleasant, white-washed farmhouse.

A middle-aged Amish woman stood on the porch, a thin smile on her lips when he emerged from the vehicle, but when her eyes fell on Amy, her entire expression warmed.

"Oh…you have a *bobbli*," she murmured, hurrying down the steps to join them.

"Hi…yes," Jacob replied quickly. "This is Amy. I'm Jacob Troyer."

"*Yah*…I know who you are." She nodded stiffly and eyed him a little too intently. "Gideon is in the living room. You can leave the *maedel* with me if you like."

"Do you have cows?" Amy asked matter-of-factly.

"We have sheep," Gideon's wife replied. "Will that do?"

Amy squeaked with pleasure and Jacob knew he had little choice but to allow his daughter to go off with the woman who happily assumed the role of caregiver.

Inhaling, Jacob made his way up the steps of the front porch as Amy toddled away and wiped his sweaty palms on the front of his jeans. He felt conspicuously out of place and wished he'd thought to dress more modestly for the encounter, but he really didn't have much else to wear.

He knocked on the door, waiting for a reply, but when no one answered, he let himself in through the screen door, calling out.

"Hello?"

"In here, Jacob," came a deep, male voice. Jacob followed the sound to the left and found a gray-haired man in a white shirt, sitting in a wing chair. His head swiveled as if to do a double take when he set his eyes on Jacob.

"Hi," Jacob offered nervously. "I-I'm Jacob Troyer."

"*Yah*, I would know you anywhere," he agreed, rising slowly. "You're the spitting image of Oscar."

It was Jacob's turn to be shocked, and he gaped at the man. "You know my grandfather?"

Gideon smiled ruefully. "I knew your *Grossdaddi* a long time ago," he replied. "Before he left the community."

Jacob swallowed, suddenly unsure if he'd made a mistake in coming.

*Did he call me here to berate me? Is he here to tell me to leave?*

A dozen terrible thoughts crossed his mind, but Gideon's next words put him at ease. "I always hoped that Oscar would return. He was devout and loved his *familye*. But he loved your *Grossmammi* more, I suppose. I can't fault a *mann* for following his heart."

Gideon gestured for Jacob to sit, and the younger man did so, the elder following his lead. "Now, I understand that you hope to rejoin the district."

"I...well, yes," Jacob fumbled. "I—my wife passed away and I have a young daughter—"

"Your situation was explained to me," Gideon interrupted gently. "It's very tragic and I think it's very noble that you want to provide a *gut* life for your *dochder*..."

Jacob stared at him expectantly, sensing a giant "but" underlying.

"However, just because your grandfather was Amish, you won't simply be accepted into the community. This isn't a place people simply wander into. Our faith is not something to be taken lightly."

Jacob nodded vehemently.

"I understand that," he agreed. "And I am willing to do whatever it takes to see us integrated as part of the community."

"In your case, it will take a great deal," Gideon warned. "You will need to learn the ways of the *Ordnung*. Do you know what that means?"

"Yes," Jacob reassured him. "The basic tenets of the faith. I believe I have learned most of them."

"You will be tested on them."

"I will be ready," he replied confidently.

"Do you speak *Deutsch* at all?" Gideon asked bluntly. Jacob pressed his lips together and hung his head.

"No…not yet, but I do speak Spanish fluently. I was a police officer in Philadelphia and I learned the language in a matter of months—on my own."

Gideon was aghast. "You worked in law enforcement?" he asked worriedly. "Do you carry a weapon?"

Jacob shook his head. "No! No, not anymore. I gave all that up after…I don't want any part of that, the violence, the crime…"

He shuddered, the memory of Nancy's bullet riddled body still too fresh in his mind. "No. I would never pick up a gun again."

"I would hope not," Gideon murmured, but there was doubt in his voice now. "We are pacifists. We don't condone or promote violence in any form."

"Nor do I," Jacob promised. "That's not the world I want for Amy."

Gideon nodded again, rubbing his hand across the long threads of his beard thoughtfully. "You have a lot of work to do before you will be considered for baptism, Jacob, but assuming you are permitted into the community, there will be other demands of you. Do you think you will be prepared to uphold them also?"

Jacob stared at him, unsure of what he meant, but didn't speak his uncertainty aloud. "I-I think I can uphold anything that is required of me," he said.

"Including remarrying?"

The question was a slap to his face.

*For people opposed to physical assault, they sure have mastered other ways of administering blows,* Jacob thought grimly. He gulped back the stone in his throat.

"I only just lost my wife," he reminded the Bishop. "Amy only just lost her mother."

"More the reason to think of finding another one for her," Gideon replied. "Of course, you couldn't remarry until you were baptized, so I am getting ahead of myself, but I want you to go into this with your eyes entirely open. This is not a decision to be made without prayer and much thought."

"I understand," Jacob said stiffly, but inside, he found himself having growing doubts.

The work, the learning of a new language and culture, giving up the luxuries he had had always felt had weighed him down were one thing. But replacing Nancy?

*I'll cross that bridge if I ever have to come to it,* he decided, knowing in his heart that he would never be ready to make that leap. His soul belonged to his lost wife. No one could ever take her place, today or a year from now.

# CHAPTER 5

Lydia had been unable to think about anything but the handsome Jacob Troyer for two days, her sleep disrupted with the anticipation.

Daniel took note of her disheveled appearance on Tuesday morning and made a comment of it over the breakfast table.

"Are you *grank*?" he asked, mortifying the young woman. She gawked at her brother as her father peered worriedly at her.

"*Nee*! Why are you asking me that?" she demanded, aghast, as she turned to face her family from the stove, wiping her hands hastily on her apron.

"You're pale and there are bags under your eyes."

"You shouldn't be around the *kinner* if you're *grank*," Simeon added, concern lacing his words. "Oh...maybe Leah can watch the *maedel* today—"

"*NEE!*" Lydia almost shouted. She did not need the neighbor watching over Amy on Jacob's first day on the job. She had been looking forward to it. Her brother and father gaped at her loud response, and she offered them a meek smile. "I mean, I'm not sick. I didn't sleep well last night. Didn't you hear the coyotes?"

The men glanced at one another in confusion and Lydia felt a pang of guilt for fibbing, but she was not about to explain that she had been unable to sleep because Jacob's face had kept her awake.

"I didn't hear anything," Simeon replied, rising from the table. "I should check on the *hinkel*!"

"I did already," Lydia reassured him, blushing as she returned to her cooking of breakfast. "The chickens are fine."

But as her head moved toward the window, her heart stopped to see the dark red minivan pulling up the driveway.

"He's here!" she gasped before she could stop herself.

"Who?" Daniel said.

"Jacob," Simeon answered for her, sounding approving. "He's earlier than I expected."

Lydia also hadn't expected him so early, but she was pleased to see him there. She turned off the stove and scraped eggs onto four plates instead of three, certain her nerves would keep her from eating now.

Through her peripheral vision, she watched the father carry his sleepy daughter toward the house, around the front.

"I'll get it," Lydia announced, rushing toward the entranceway.

"What has gotten into her this morning?" she heard her brother ask behind her. "Are you sure she's not sick?"

Lydia ignored their concerns and threw open the door before Jacob could knock. Amy turned her head from her father's shoulder as Jacob smiled warmly, recognition lighting his face.

"Hi!" Amy screeched, the tiredness gone from her face as her pretty eyes fell on Lydia.

"*Hallo, liebling,*" Lydia said sweetly. To her endearment, Amy extended her arms toward Lydia and Jacob struggled to keep his child in his hold.

"No, Amy—"

"It's all right," Lydia reassured him. "I don't mind."

Reluctantly, Jacob handed his eager daughter into Lydia's open arms. Immediately, the woman was consumed with a warmth like she had never known, flooding her from head to toe as Amy clung to her neck.

"Can we see the animals?" Amy whispered loudly in her ear.

"*Yah*, we can," Lydia agreed. "I have many things planned for us *heit*—today."

"*Yah. Heit,*" Amy repeated, giggling with the new words. Lydia's smile hurt her face, her eyes locking on Jacob's, but their gaze was short-lived as Daniel and Simeon emerged from the kitchen.

"*Hallo*, Jacob," Simeon called. "This is Daniel, my *suh*—my son."

Warily, Lydia turned to see how her brother would address the Englisher, but to her surprise, her sibling offered the newcomer a broad grin. "Finally, some *hilf* around here, *Daed*," Daniel chortled.

Simeon rolled his eyes. "Let's get to it, *yah?*"

Jacob hesitated, eying his daughter again. "Amy, you listen to Lydia, okay?"

"We'll be fine," Lydia reassured him. "Won't we, Amy?"

"What animals?" Amy demanded. "Sheep? I seed baa-baa's yesterday."

Lydia raised an eyebrow, her heart skipping as she realized where Amy might have seen such creatures. Again, her eyes fell on Jacob, but he was already being herded off by Simeon and Daniel.

"We don't have sheep," she told Amy, making her way back into the kitchen. "But I will show you around the farm after you have *mariyeesse*. Do you know what that is?"

Amy shook her head.

"Breakfast. Have you had breakfast yet?"

Amy nodded. "I had a Pop Tart!" she declared proudly, and Lydia grimaced.

"That's not much of a breakfast for a growing girl," Lydia told her firmly, setting the child on the seat that her brother had previously occupied. "What about some eggs and bacon? Do you like eggs?"

Amy nodded, her pretty irises shining in the morning light. "I like eggs. They come from chickies."

Lydia laughed, her auburn head turning back toward the counter to collect one of the plates. The men filed by the window as she did, and she silently bid Jacob a good first day. It was bound to be a difficult one for him, but she had faith that he could do it.

She would be praying for him to make it through.

~

Amy proved to be an inquisitive and well-behaved child, considering her circumstances. Lydia had expected some resistance from her given the way her life had been uprooted, her father moving her away from her home in the city, but Amy was too enthralled with farming.

Endless childish questions sprung from her lips, and Lydia was happy to answer them all.

"What's that?" Constantly piped from the toddler's lips, her little mouth repeating the words, often in Pennsylvania Dutch, when Lydia spoke them. Sparks of pride ignited inside Lydia as she realized she was doing her own small part to ensure that Jacob found his way back into the community, which was their birthright.

*Did he meet with the Bishop? Is that where Amy saw the sheep yesterday?*

Lydia knew the Kauffmans owned sheep. She had spoken to the elder about Jacob's situation in hopes that he would get in touch with the man about it. She just had not expected it to have occurred so soon.

*Did it go well? I wonder what the Bishop said.*

At noon, Lydia had a difficult time wrangling Amy back to the house, where she fixed sandwiches for the men, hard at work.

"I want to play with the animals!" Amy protested.

"And we will," Lydia promised. "But your *vadder* and mine are *hungerich*. Don't you want to make sure they've eaten?"

There was no appealing to a small child with a one-track mind, but in the end, Amy agreed to help Lydia on the condition that they immediately return to the livestock.

"We'll deliver the *esse* to the *mannsleit* and then we'll go back to see the animals," Lydia chuckled, not wanting to quash the girl's infectious enthusiasm.

But when Lydia and Amy found Jacob out in the fields, her amusement died away. Sweat poured down his face, his skin sunburned despite the low intensity of the rays that day.

"Uh oh," Amy intoned when she saw him. "Daddy tired."

"I'm fine," Jacob gasped, accepting a thermos of water gratefully from Lydia. Daniel turned through a row of corn and burst into laughter at the sight of the new worker.

"Are you going to drop, Jake?" he teased. Lydia frowned at her brother, but he did not seem to notice as he neared the others, his grin overtaking his face.

"I'm good. I-I'm just getting my bearings," Jacob insisted, embarrassment coloring his face. "Have I done something wrong?"

Daniel looked at the rows of corn among them and shook his head. "*Nee*. It all looks *gut*," he replied. Pride sparked in Jacob's eyes as he wiped his face with his hands, sweat falling over his work shirt. For the first time, Lydia realized he was dressed in homespun clothes, not English outfits.

*I wonder where he found those.*

"I brought sandwiches," Lydia announced, holding up the picnic basket in her hands. "Where's *Daed*?"

"Mucking out the barn," Daniel replied. "I'll take him something to *esse*."

He reached for the basket, but Lydia removed a sandwich for Jacob first, offering it to him. He took it gratefully as her brother vanished with the others.

"Are you all right?" Lydia asked softly when her brother was out of earshot. "You do look ready to drop."

Amy had wandered through the corn, but Lydia was unconcerned. At Amy's age, she had done the same thing, as had Daniel. The land had raised them as much as their father had in the wake of their mother's passing when Daniel was three.

"I'm fine," Jacob said again, a note of defensiveness lining his words, but Lydia offered him a compassionate smile.

"I'm not going to report back to my *vadder* and *bruder* if you tell me the truth," she reassured him. "The *warrick* is hard. I know that as well as anyone."

Jacob eyed her warily, but his shoulders sagged as if he were lowering his guard and he nodded. "The work—*warrick*—is hard," he agreed quietly. "But I just need to find my groove. I'll get there."

"I have no doubt that you will. If Daniel said you've done well, then you must be doing well."

His face brightened. "Yeah?"

Lydia nodded encouragingly. "He's not free with his compliments. But don't push yourself too hard, too fast. You won't be any good to anyone if you end up exhausted or injured."

"I won't," he vowed. "I've done intensive training before as…"

He trailed off and bit his lower lip as if stopping himself from spilling a secret. "I've done hard work before. I just need to find my groove, like I said."

Jacob offered her a small smile and took another swig of the water. "I really appreciate you watching over Amy, by the way. I'll pay you when I get paid—"

"Nonsense!" Lydia interrupted, shocked that he would offer. "That's—we don't do things like that here."

Jacob stared at her, embarrassed. "I'm sorry," he muttered. "I didn't mean to offend you, but you shouldn't watch a stranger's kid for nothing."

"But you're not a stranger, are you, Jake?" she demurred softly. "You're one of us."

Their eyes met and Lydia's pulse raced as he studied her face, curiosity overcoming him.

"You called on the Bishop for me," he breathed, glancing over his shoulder. Lydia nodded, heat tinging her cheeks.

"Then—*denki* for that."

Her dark eyebrows rose. "Did it go well?" she asked, pleasure surging through her. "You met with him already?"

"I'm not sure if it went well, per se, but we did meet and he's willing to entertain the idea of us starting a life here—if I can make it through the long list of protocols."

Lydia frowned. "Like what?"

"Like…learning the *Ordnung* and the language."

She giggled softly. "I can help you with those things," she promised.

"Yeah? You would do that?"

"Of course. Amy is already learning some words. Maybe she can teach you some *dienacht*." She leaned closer and whispered, "That means 'tonight'."

Jacob began to chuckle. "Yes—*yah*! I figured that out."

Lydia beamed at him. "If you stay on here and absorb the way we talk, how we act and attend worship, I think you'll have a good sense for our ways in no time at all."

"I hope you're right. You make it sound so easy when yesterday it seemed so insurmountable."

"Nothing is insurmountable if you really want it," Lydia told him wisely.

Jacob grinned. "How did you get so smart in your twenty years?" he teased. A blush stained her face completely red now.

"I'm a little older than that," she mumbled, turning away to find his daughter. "Don't lose faith, Jake."

"I don't think I can now, Lydia," he replied lightly.

"Lydie, stop distracting the *bu*!" Simeon yelled out from somewhere she could not see. Her cheeks were so hot, she worried the skin might peel away from the flesh.

"I should go," Lydia muttered, careful to keep her crimson complexion away from him.

"See you later."

*I can't wait,* Lydia thought, hurrying off.

# CHAPTER 6

Although it wasn't terribly late when Jacob collected Amy and left the farm, the little girl was exhausted from the day's events and fell asleep in her car seat on the way back to the hotel.

"She wouldn't nap," Lydia had said apologetically when he went to get the child. "She was too excited about the animals."

"That's all right." Jacob chuckled. "Hopefully, she'll sleep the night away then."

He gathered her in his arms when they arrived at their room, but Amy didn't stir, her tiredness infectious after the day Jacob had experienced. Every muscle in his body ached, and he was starving.

*Looks like we're ordering another pizza,* he thought glumly. The memory of Lydia's thick ham sandwich lingered on his tongue, and he wished he were sitting at a dinner table with her instead of calling for takeout again.

*Is it her food I'm missing or Lydia?*

He shook off the intrusive question and stripped off his clothes, determined to shower before the pizza arrived. He gave Amy a final glance before disappearing into the bathroom, leaving the door open slightly in case his daughter woke up.

Scrubbing the grime and tiredness from his skin, Jacob once more found himself thinking of Lydia, despite his best efforts to block her lovely, compassionate face from his mind.

*She's been so kind to me for no reason at all,* he thought, soaping himself and lathering with vigor as if to wash away the thoughts that he had no business feeling. She would make a very good friend in the district, and that's what Jacob needed now. Friends. Nothing more.

The motel's hot water reserve wasn't deep and soon the spray turned cold, forcing him out of the shower. He hastily dressed into a pair of old track pants and plain t-shirt, pulling out the second work outfit he had bought for the farm. He would need to find a laundromat soon to keep up with the mounting pile of laundry.

And a suitable place to live.

No matter what happened with his baptism, he and Amy could not live in the motel forever. It wasn't financially, nor logically, feasible.

*I can't raise my daughter like this. It's counterproductive to what I've been trying to do—grant her security.*

Sighing deeply, Jacob slipped onto the twin bed where Amy slept and gently brushed her blonde curls away from her chubby cheeks. Her rosebud lips gaped slightly, eyes moving beneath her lids in the throes of a dream.

"You just need to hang in there a bit longer, okay, peanut?" he murmured, more to himself than the slumbering girl. "Daddy's going to figure this out for us."

The shrill ring of his cell phone startled him and with a sigh, Jacob swung his legs over the side of the bed to grab it before it could wake up his daughter. The blocked number would have usually deterred him from answering, but he was sure it was the pizza man.

"Hello?" he rasped in a low voice, one eye on his child. For half a second, there was no response and dread snaked down Jacob's neck as he realized his mistake.

"Where the hell are you?" Billy growled before Jacob could disconnect the call.

*Dammit! Why did I pick up?*

It wasn't too late to hang up, but it would only open the floodgate of calls again, calls that Jacob had finally thought he had put an end to.

"That's none of your concern, Billy," Jacob replied flatly. "I told you that the last time we spoke—you and your mother."

"My mother is Amy's grandmother!" Billy yelled. Jacob jerked the phone away from his ear, his heart beginning to race.

"And I'm her father. I'll always do what's best for my daughter."

"You think that keeping Amy from her family is what's best for her? Have you completely lost your mind!"

Jacob inhaled sharply, refusing to be provoked by his brother-in-law. "I tried to have a relationship with all of you but you tried to take Amy from me," he reminded Billy tautly.

"I'm not going to sit idly by and let Clarissa use her bottomless pit of money to fight for custody of my daughter for no reason other than spite."

"Spite?! You're acting like a maniac! You just packed up your house and left without telling anyone where you were going? Mom could clearly see there was something wrong with you—"

"Don't give me that," Jacob hissed. "I didn't tell you anything because I didn't want any of you knowing where to find us. Which is completely within my rights after the way you've been acting."

"It's your fault Nancy's dead!" Billy howled, his words piercing through Jacob's soul. "She should have never married a cop! We warned her about you!"

"Nancy was collateral damage in a gang fight," Jacob said dully. "It had nothing to do with me."

"It was probably revenge for someone you put away or—"

"It wasn't," Jacob interrupted again, his head beginning to pound at the same fight with Billy he'd had at least a dozen times over the past year. "And I don't know how many more investigations you need to see that."

"You and your buddies at the police department are all one big wall of blue silence!" Billy screamed, again forcing Jacob to pull the phone away from his ear. "Bring Amy home. NOW!"

"Amy is never coming back to Philadelphia and neither am I. In fact, I doubt you'll ever see me again. If you see her, that will be her choice when she's old enough to make it."

Billy choked, as if Jacob had genuinely offended him. "I can't believe you would be that heartless!"

"I tried with you. I tried, for Amy's sake, but you and your family just made it ugly and impossible to grieve for Nancy. I can only assume it was because your grief was so heavy, but now I know that's not for me to sit back and take. Goodbye, Billy."

"Don't you dare hang up on me, Jake! Don't you dare! This is cruel! My mom lost her only daughter!"

"And her solution is to take mine?"

Billy fell silent for a moment, as if considering Jacob's words. But when he spoke again, his tone was anything but sensible.

"BRING HER BACK RIGHT NOW OR I'LL HIRE A PI TO FIND YOU!"

Amy stirred in her bed, her uncle's shrieking finally getting through to the room.

"Bye, Billy." Jacob hung up, but before he set the phone aside, he did what he should have done months ago.

Block contact.

Block contact.

Block contact.

All three of Nancy's immediate family members were firewalled into oblivion, no longer apt to bother Jacob through their regular numbers.

*Not that it will stop Billy and Clarissa from trying to reach out in other ways.*

Setting the device back on the nightstand, Jacob bit on his lower lip and looked skyward apologetically.

*I'm sorry, Nancy. I really did try with your family, but they wanted to take Amy. I can't stand for that.*

Headlights flashed outside the window, and Jacob nervously stood to peer into the parking lot. A young man let himself out of the driver's side of a tiny, red car, pizza warmer in hand, and Jacob's shoulders relaxed as he moved to answer the door with a twenty-dollar bill in hand.

"Thanks," Jacob whispered. "Keep the change."

The driver grinned and waved, hurrying back to his vehicle while Jacob secured the door with a deadbolt. Setting the pizza on the table, he suddenly wasn't hungry anymore as he stared at his sleeping child.

*We really do need to find better accommodations than this,* he thought worriedly. *For more reasons than the obvious one.*

Pizza for supper and the motel room fees were eating up every dime he had, but rent cost money too. And he would need to put his name on a lease if he wanted to find an apartment. What if Billy did follow through with his threat to hire a private investigator? Putting his name on a lease would lead anyone looking directly to his doorstep.

*My credit card is on this room too. That will do the same thing.*

He was thankful for his police background in that moment, knowing exactly what it would take for someone to find him if they were looking. At that moment, he would be easily located.

*But why does that matter? What can Clarissa and Billy really do if they do come here?*

Maybe Clarissa didn't have a leg to stand on, taking custody of Amy, but having the Winston family in Calico when he was trying to prove himself to the Amish community wouldn't be helpful in the least. Not to mention Billy's volatility roused a dark side of Jacob too.

No. Jacob didn't need the Winstons anywhere near Lancaster County. He would need to go off-grid.

But how without any cash on hand?

He decided he would talk to Lydia about it in the morning when he went back to work. She had promised to help him, and, so far, she had been the best friend he had found in Calico. Maybe she would have some solutions to this problem.

Jacob just had to swallow his pride and ensure that he asked her.

## CHAPTER 7

*J*acob's bones ached to their marrow, but he didn't slow down for a second, the final load from the motel packed in the back of the minivan, the keys turned into Mara after ten days of living in the motel.

*And not a minute too soon.*

He was genuinely unsure if he would have been able to foot another week of living under those conditions financially. There was no more money in his savings account, every penny he was earning going directly to takeout food and paying the bill for the room.

"Is this our *haus*, Daddy?" Amy asked for the fourth time that day. He looked at her, perched in her car seat, kicking her simple black boots against the seat as she cocked her blonde curls. She looked like a picture in the modest blue dress that Lydia had sewn for her, seemingly out of thin air. One day after his work on the farm, Amy had been wearing it, along with a huge smile on her face.

"Is it, Daddy?" Amy asked again, and they both looked at the pretty little structure in front of them. Daniel and another man wrestled with a mattress through the front door of the single-storey home, set back on the Hertzler property, tucked below the hill next to the main house.

"*Yah*, Amy. You already knew that we were moving here."

"Are you going to sit there all day while we do all the *warrick*?" Daniel called out from the doorway, a grimace twisted over his face. A moment later, Lydia appeared from inside the *dawdi haus*, followed by Annie, the women hurrying to the car as Jacob jumped out to join the men.

"*Hallo, liebling*," Annie sang when she saw Amy, but Jacob caught Lydia's friends sidelong look. "Look how big you've gotten in only a few days!"

Lydia helped the girl from the car as Jacob opened the back to unload the rest of their belongings. He gave Annie another grateful look. "You have no idea how much this means to us—" he started to say, but Annie waved her hand dismissively, scooping Amy into her arms.

"Now, you have to stop with that, Jake," Annie chided him gently. "That is what we do for each other. We had a *dawdi haus* that is only collecting dust. A *maedel* shouldn't live in a motel room, *yah*? And now you can get to *warrick* even earlier in the *mariye*."

Annie giggled as Lydia gasped. "Annie!"

"He gets there early enough!" Daniel called out and Annie turned her head toward him.

"It must be nice to have someone to share the *warrick* with, Danny," Annie called sweetly, fluttering her eyes, but Daniel had already resumed his struggle with the mattress, leaving Annie looking frustrated.

"*Wat* is wrong with your *bruder*?" she grumbled, marching away with Amy in her arms. Lydia swallowed a smile and fixed her attention on the van, reaching for a plastic tote to carry inside the *dawdi haus*.

"Her *familye* is very kind for opening their home to us," Jacob told Lydia in a low voice. "Even if she is brushing it off as if it's nothing."

Lydia stopped and shook her head. "They wouldn't do it if they weren't able, Jake. Elias was the one who suggested it when I started asking around about rooms for rent."

"I appreciate it, all the same."

Lydia gave him a tentative smile. "Annie is right about one thing; having you closer will make studying much easier. After the chores are done, we could work on language lessons…if you want."

Jacob nodded vehemently. "I do want! Very much!"

Relief colored Lydia's face, and she grinned happily. "We could start tomorrow, after *warrick*. I could *komme* and cook *nachtesse* and we could go over some exercises…"

She trailed off, paling as if she had overstepped her place. For a second, Jacob merely looked at her.

*Like a date? Can I have another woman cooking me dinner?*

But was Lydia some other woman, cooking him dinner? She had been a true friend, helping him when no one else had believed in him.

"*Es dutt mer leed…*" she mumbled.

"You have nothing to be sorry about," Jacob interrupted quickly, finding his voice. "I must have zoned out there for a minute. *Yah*. I would like that very much, *denki*. *Nachtesse*, tomorrow night.

Happiness flooded Lydia's face, but she did her best to hide it as she bowed her chin and turned away with his box from the car.

*Am I leading her on? I can't offer her anything, can I?*

But he didn't cancel the plans, either. He was secretly looking forward to a home cooked meal for once in far too long.

∽

"Jake is late this *mariye*," Simeon commented, peering up at the clock over the kitchen window. Lydia glanced upward too, fanning herself with a tea towel in the process. The July heat was already scorching at that early hour, the humidity creeping into the kitchen with dawn's early rays.

"He's not late," she protested as a fission of alarm sparked in her gut. Her father was right: he was later than usual.

"You were *deheem* later than usual last *nacht*, too," Daniel teased. "Maybe that's why he's so late."

Lydia gaped at him indignantly as Simeon gave his son a reproving look. "Don't be crass, Danny."

"I wasn't! Everyone knows they're courting, *Daed*!" Daniel argued, pouting slightly at the reprimand.

Lydia's cheeks turned purple with embarrassment as her father gawked at her now. "*Wat!*"

"*Nee*! We're not! That's just gossip!" she protested. She did not add that she wished it were true, but that Jacob was very slow to make his move. That did not change the fact that they spent almost every waking hour in each other's company, between his work at the Yoder's farm and his studying under Lydia's tutelage.

"He's not considered part of the community yet, Lydia," Simeon warned her. "You tread carefully."

She frowned and eyed her father, unaccustomed to challenging him but curious all the same.

"He works and lives among us," she reminded him. "He's made *freind* and attends worship like anyone else who hasn't been baptized."

"He's not fluent in the language yet," Daniel piped in unhelpfully. Lydia cast her brother a reproachful look.

"He studies so hard every day while caring for his *dochder*, *Daed*. You know how hard that is. You did it yourself. Why are you being so judgmental?"

Simeon appeared hurt by her accusation.

"It's not judgement in the least. If I thought negatively about Jake, I wouldn't have allowed him to work here, let alone permitted you to spend so much time with him and Amy. My only concern is for you."

Confused, Lydia turned fully toward him, leaning against the counter. "I don't understand," she said slowly.

"He only just lost his *weib*, Lydia, the *mudder* of his *kinner*. That is a difficult time for any *mann*—trust me when I tell you this. He has moved his child away from the only city he's ever known…that is a lot of change for one *mann* to endure. He may be overwhelmed with changes."

*Or maybe this is Daed's way of saying that he thinks I'm too bookish for Jake, just like all the other mannsleit he knows.*

"I think it would be much wiser if you both keep whatever feelings you might develop on hold until after Jake's baptism."

"If he gets baptized," Daniel quipped. Lydia ignored her brother and stared at her father's worried face. It was difficult to tell what was truly worrying him the most. But if Jacob were to confess his feelings for her, she was not sure she would be able to hold off for months, if not another year, to reciprocate.

*Of course, he would need to tell me how he feels about me first.*

"Oh, *Daed*—" She abruptly stopped speaking when a buggy rolled up the driveway, a single horse pulling it along awkwardly. "Who is that?"

Both men rose from the table to join her at the window, and, in unison, the trio gasped and laughed. "Jake!"

The Yoders hurried toward the front door to greet Jacob, who seemed to have a difficult time slowing his horse, their amusement palpable.

"*Hilf* him, Danny!" Lydia urged when she stopped giggling. Her brother jumped into action and slowed the horse down, the beast snorting and spitting in protest as Amy squealed in delight from the back of the buggy.

"Again, Daddy! Again!"

"No!" Jacob grumbled, dismounting. He pulled his daughter from the back, her little fingers locking on his suspenders, her golden crown knocking on the brim of his straw hat.

"Please, Daddy? Horsie ride!"

"Where is your car?" Lydia asked, reaching for Amy, who willingly thrust herself into the woman's embrace.

"No car. Horsie," Amy eloquently explained. Lydia and Simeon stared at Jacob in disbelief.

"I sold the van and…" he gestured behind him at the buggy.

"You should have told me," Daniel complained, examining the buggy. "I would have gone with you."

Jacob cast Lydia a sidelong look. "I wanted it to be a surprise."

*For me?* she wondered, her chest tightening with excitement. She tried not to read too much into the words and look.

"I think you did very well. She's a beautiful horse," Lydia offered.

"Her name is Peanut," Amy announced.

Lydia beamed. "Isn't that what your *vadder* calls you?"

"*Yah*, and now I can call her Peanut."

"That seems like a very fair trade," Lydia told her, readjusting the girl on her hip. "*Komme* inside and *esse*. Breakfast is getting *kald*."

∼

After the day's chores were done, Jacob took Lydia aside and asked if they might leave Amy with Annie for an hour. Lydia's heart swelled in anticipation.

"Oh?" she replied, her voice squeaking. "Why?"

Jacob shuffled his boots uncomfortably, glancing at the ground as he ran a hand through his thick head of hair.

"I-I was hoping you could give me proper driving lessons," he admitted. Lydia tried not to feel disappointed but focussed on the fact that they would be spending time alone together for the first time. Amy had always been with them previously.

"I'm sure Annie would enjoy keeping her for a little while," Lydia reassured him. "Let me ask her."

With Amy squared away at Annie's, Lydia took the reins and guided the buggy to a quiet area with a flat, open field, which she knew would allow for a good starter course.

"I feel bad that I'm always asking so much of you, Lydie," Jacob confessed when they parked. "You can always feel free to say no, you know?"

Lydia raised her head. "Why would I say no?" she asked, genuinely confused.

"Because I don't want to take advantage of your goodness."

Her lower lip dropped slightly, and she shifted her gaze. "Are you?"

"*Wat?*"

"Taking advantage of me?"

"I really hope not," Jacob murmured, sounding pained. "But I can't help but feel like I'm taking more than I'm giving."

"That's the way of the world, Jake. Sometimes it's your time to give and others it's your time to receive. You just need to remember to balance the scales when it's right."

She smiled weakly and raised her head again, suddenly distinctly aware of how close his face was to hers. The wisp of his breath against her face sent shivers through her, but before Lydia could dare to hope for the kiss she had dreamt of, Jacob abruptly pulled back and cleared his throat.

"Okay, so what am I doing wrong with this thing?" he asked, his voice a tad too loud. Again, swallowing her disappointment, Lydia settled back against the bench and began to teach him how to sit and hold the reins, ignoring how close he was to her.

*Is Daed right? Is he afraid to move on after the loss of his weib? Or does he just think of me as a friend?*

Their near kiss had certainly indicated stronger feelings than friendship, but now, Lydia was in a state of inner conflict. She vowed to pray for guidance on how to best approach matters with Jacob that night. After all, the last time she had prayed on matters of the heart, Jacob had dropped directly on her doorstep.

"You are getting this," Lydia said and laughed, half an hour later, Peanut trotting obediently and stopping on command to Jacob's tugs.

"It's really not that hard when you have a *gut* teacher," he teased, winking. Lydia blushed.

"We should get back. Amy will be getting tired and we haven't eaten yet."

She caught the adoring look he offered her as he nodded. "She really likes you, Lydie. She talks about you all morning when we're on our way to the *bauerie*."

"She's a very special *maedel*. But I think she likes the *wutz* more than me."

Jacob scoffed and laughed in disbelief.

"She does not like the pigs at all, actually," he corrected as they headed back toward the Hertzler property. "But you might be a tie for the chickens."

Giggling, the pair trotted Peanut back, Jacob in the driver's seat this time, his confidence radiating after one quick lesson.

But as they neared the Hertzler house, Jacob slowed the horse, his smile fading away to a thin line.

"Jake?" Lydia asked worriedly, following his gaze. "What's wrong?"

Her eyes fell on a huge vehicle parked on the tall grass outside of Annie's house, the tires almost as big as the truck itself.

"W-who is that?" Jacob croaked.

"I have no idea," Lydia answered honestly.

"Oh, no..." Jacob whispered and suddenly, the buggy was flying toward the house, the pair flying with it as Lydia gasped.

"Jake, slow down!" she yelped. "What's wrong?"

His jaw clenched, the bone twitching as he leaned forward, his entire body shaking. When they came to a stop, he whipped his head around to Lydia.

"Go home," he urged.

"*Wat? Nee!*" she replied, but he was already scrambling off the bench, sprinting toward the front of Annie's house. "JAKE!"

The front door opened, and Annie emerged, her face pale as her father exited behind her. Behind him, an obese Englisher pushed through both of them, pulling a screaming Amy by the hand.

"Well, look who decided to show up," the stranger spat over Amy's wails. "I told you I'd find you, Jake."

# CHAPTER 8

Amy's tears, and seeing Billy handling his daughter with such aggression, colored Jacob's vision red. He rushed toward the pair without thinking as Annie and her father tried to put themselves between the irate man and the Englisher.

"Let my daughter go, Billy," Jacob hissed from between clenched teeth. Amy's screams took on a fever pitch, and she began to wriggle out of her uncle's grasp, finally managing to get away and make it into her father's relieved arms. Jacob scooped her up, his heart in his throat.

"Get back here, Amy. I'm taking you home, to your grandma, honey," Billy cooed placatingly as she settled down some now that she was out of his hold. "Don't you remember me?"

"How would she remember you, Billy?" Jacob spat furiously. "She hasn't seen you in months!"

"And whose fault is that!" Jacob's brother-in-law roared, his voice carrying over the fields to tense everyone in earshot.

"Keep your voice down," Jacob told him sternly, pressing Amy's sobbing face to his chest. Lydia tapped his shoulder and reached for the girl, who eagerly took to her hold.

"Lydia, you should go *deheem*," he told her in a low voice, unsure of what might transpire in front of the young woman.

"You're Amish, now?" Billy cawed in disbelief, nodding at Jacob's clothes. "Are you kidding me?"

"My grandfather was a part of this community," Jacob informed him, hating that he felt the need to explain himself. "I have every right to be here."

"You're hiding," Billy countered. "And indoctrinating Amy with this Bible-thumping crap."

Anger exploded in Jacob's veins, a familiar feeling when dealing with his brother-in-law.

"You don't know anything about faith and community," he growled. "And I won't have you trash talking these good people."

"I don't give a rat's ass what you do, but don't drag Amy into it. This is just more fuel for our court case against you. You never were fit to be a parent. I warned Nancy about you. I knew you would be a terrible husband and worse father."

Jacob felt his hands ball into fists at his side, but before he could respond or react, Annie's father spoke.

"*Yung mann*, you're not welcome on our property," Elias told him firmly. "*Pliese,* take your truck and leave. Do not return here."

"I'm not leaving here without my niece. My mother is in that one-horse town waiting for word. As soon as the private investigator told us that you'd sold your car, we had you at this address."

The glee in his tone churned Jacob's stomach.

"You will leave here or I'll have the Sheriff sent for," Elias insisted. "You have no right to be on my land."

Billy balked at the mention of law enforcement, doubt clouding his eyes. He had been arrested enough times to not welcome another one.

"I know where to find you now," Billy warned, scowling at them all. "You haven't heard the last of me."

With a final glare, he spun around toward his truck and got inside, revving the engine unnecessarily high before peeling out of the yard, kicking up dirt to spray over the lawn and disappearing down the country road.

Jacob didn't realize he was shaking until Lydia placed a hand on his shoulder.

"Are you all right?" she asked, worried, balancing Amy on her hip. Not trusting his voice, he scooped his daughter from her arms and embraced her tightly, swallowing the lump of fear in his throat.

"Who was that, Jake?" Elias asked nervously. "Why was he so angry?"

"*Es dutt mer leed*," Jacob managed to apologize weakly. "He… he is my late *weib's bruder*."

"What was all that about?" Annie demanded, her eyes dancing uncertainly from Lydia to Jacob.

His mind was reeling from the encounter, shame overcoming him. He had brought trouble to the district, to these kind people who had gone out of their way to help him. He had to make other arrangements for when Billy returned because he had no doubt that his brother-in-law would be back.

"He..." Jacob inhaled shakily and collected his thoughts. "He blames me for his sister's death in some way. I..."

"*Wat?*" Lydia was baffled, but Annie stepped in.

"*Komme. Hoch dich anne.*" The blonde woman ushered the others toward the seats on the porch as Jacob calmed his daughter, wiping away her tears.

"I don't wanna go with than *mann*, Daddy."

"You're not going anywhere, peanut," he told her firmly, his pulse racing as he prayed he was telling her the truth.

"Why does he think you're responsible for...?" Lydia trailed off, not wanting to say the words in front of Amy.

"Amy, why don't you go play with the *hinkel, yah?*" Jacob encouraged her, hoping to spare her some of the sordid details of her mother's passing.

The mention of chickens cheered her up, as always.

"Now? It's almost dark," Amy said, her eyes brightening.

"Just for a few minutes before we *esse, yah?*"

Amy did not need to be asked again, and she scampered off his lap to frolic with the fowl as the adults spoke.

"In Philadelphia, I was a police officer," Jacob confessed, avoiding their expressions as he spoke. Their faces were an identical shade of shocked. "My job was taxing and saw some of the worst atrocities that mankind could offer."

"What does that have to do with your *weib*?" Annie pressed.

"*Nix*," Jacob replied. "But Billy has convinced himself that because Nancy was shot, it was some act of revenge, despite the fact that an internal investigation proved it was just a terrible circumstance of gang violence. Nancy and Amy were caught in the crossfire…"

He choked on the words, the memory still too fresh to rehash. "Billy is just looking for someone to blame. He and his mother tried to take Amy from me almost as soon as Nancy died. They hired lawyers and tried to paint me as an unfit father. I was out of my mind with grief and fighting off all these accusations…"

"Oh, Jake…" Lydia whispered. "How awful. Why didn't you tell me?"

"I really didn't think they would ever find us out here. I had hoped to start a better life for both of us. I hoped that their anger would eventually fizzle out, but…"

He raised his head and shook it. "I'm sorry, Elias, Annie… Lydia. I'll make other arrangements. Tonight. We won't put you in harm's way again. If I'd ever thought—"

"*Wat?*" Elias cut him off. "*Wat* are you talking about?"

Jacob returned his stare. "You were here. You heard what he said, Elias. He's going to come back. Billy always follows through on his threats. Him and Clarissa really believe they have a claim to Amy."

"But they don't," Lydia said firmly. "And if he returns, you will reason with him, and he'll see how wrong he is."

"Your home is here," Annie agreed. "You're not going anywhere. You can't keep running with your *dochder* every time there's trouble, Jake. Amy needs stability, and this is not stable."

More guilt washed through him. "I can't bring problems to you," he insisted.

"You really aren't understanding our way of life, even after all these weeks, are you?" Lydia told him sadly. "We take care of one another. We don't turn our backs on each other when there are problems."

Jacob pursed his lips, not speaking his mind aloud, but Lydia seemed to sense it all the same.

"And, *yah*, Jake, you are one of us. You *esse* and *warrick* with us. You live among us and we adore you *kinner*. You are one of us and we will watch out for you and Amy. You will stay."

Jacob looked at Lydia, his heart tightening as he realized just how much he cared for her.

*How could I have let guilt keep me from her when someone so wonderful has been in front of me all this time? I won't let another moment pass me without her knowing exactly how I feel about her.*

"What if he returns?" Jacob pressed. "He's going to kick up a fuss."

"We'll deal with that if the time comes," Annie said firmly. "In the meantime, we'll all pray that Billy finds the peace he so desperately needs."

"*Komme*," Lydia urged. "It really is getting late, and Amy needs to *esse* before going to bed. Moreover, we might lose her in the *hinkel* coop if we let go much longer."

Everyone chuckled at the thought, and Jacob rose, nodding in agreement. "Are you sure?" he asked, focussing his gaze on

Elias, who ultimately had the final say on whether he stayed or went.

"I trust your days of violence are those of the past?" Elias asked thoughtfully. "You have no more police officer tendencies?"

Jacob balked at the thought. "You couldn't pay me a million dollars to return to that life."

"It's less about the payment and more about the feeling," Elias explained gently. "Would you let your temper overwhelm you? Because that is more unacceptable."

Jacob gulped and shook his head, but he could not help but remember how much Billy riled him up. So many times he had wanted to set his brother-in-law straight.

"I won't put my hands on Billy or anyone else," he vowed honestly. "I am fully committed to the *Ordnung*. Always."

Elias nodded once.

"Then you are welcome to stay on. I'll alert the neighbors to this potential problem and we will confront any issues together going forward."

"He'll tire himself out and go home when he realizes that he can't take Amy," Lydia added optimistically, stepping off the porch to find the toddler.

*She has more faith in the outcome than I do,* Jacob thought grimly, but he didn't say that aloud.

"*Guten nacht*, Annie, Elias," he called, hurrying to catch up with Lydia, who had made her way toward the chicken coop. "Lydia!"

She turned to face him curiously and, ensuring that they were out of view of her friend and Elias, he suddenly swooped in to place a long, sweet kiss on her lips.

Lydia gasped at the unexpectedness of the gesture, her eyes popping before half-closing. Jacob drew back, a small smile lingering on his lips.

"I'm sorry," he murmured. "I should have done that a long time ago."

She exhaled and giggled nervously. Her cheeks red against the darkening sky. "*Yah*," she agreed. "You should have. But it was worth the wait."

Grinning at one another, they moved toward the *dawdi haus*, calling out for Amy who immediately showed herself, her earlier upset forgotten.

*Never mind Billy. He can't stay here forever, but Amy and I are here for good. I just have to wait out his tornado temper and we can go back to building our lives.*

# CHAPTER 9

Oddly, there was no word from Billy or Clarissa over the next three days. The silence should have made Jacob uncomfortable or worried, but his budding romance with Lydia took the edge off the concern when his brother-in-law didn't materialize after the third day.

"Do you suppose they went back home already?" Lydia asked when Jacob went to collect Amy on the third day after work. Jacob tensed at the mention of Billy.

"I don't want to think about him," he admitted. "Out of sight, out of mind."

"Do you really believe that, though?" Lydia pressed, ushering Amy out the door. "You said he's not the kind of *mann* who would give up easily."

Jacob sighed and led the pair toward his waiting buggy. "Honestly, I think they probably met with a lawyer again and got told the same thing they were told in Philly—that they can't just take a kid away from their parent."

"But aren't you curious to know where they are?" Lydia pressed as they climbed into the buggy.

Amy slipped into the back and Jacob turned to Lydia. "Honestly? I'm so consumed with what's in front of me, I don't really have time to think about Billy or Clarissa. I've been praying for them."

Lydia raised an eyebrow and Jacob laughed. "I have been! Honestly. Maybe that's why they haven't been around. Maybe *Gott* heard my prayers and has sent them off to harass someone else."

He grinned wickedly, but Lydia didn't return his smile. "Do you think that one day Amy can have a relationship with her *familye*?"

Jacob's smile faded, and he turned away, grabbing for the reins. "I've always wanted that for her," he muttered, annoyed that Lydia would think otherwise. "It wasn't me who made this so difficult."

"I know that. It's just so sad for her."

"When she's old enough, if she wants to go and meet her uncle and grandparents, I won't stand in her way. I think Nancy would have wanted that for her. But they want to kidnap her, Lydia."

"I think you're doing the right thing for her," Lydia reassured him, reaching for his free hand. "I'm not judging you."

"Hey!"

They turned toward the house as Daniel came rushing out, his face flushed. "Oh, *gut*, I caught you."

Jacob cocked his head to the side. "*Wat* is it, Danny?"

"Can I catch a ride into town with you? *Daed* took the buggy to market and I'm stranded."

"You could walk," Lydia teased.

"We're going into town," Jacob scolded her laughingly. "*Yah*, get in. Where are you going?"

"Games night at the community center," Daniel informed them.

"Oh, *yah*? Annie is going there too," Lydia said. Daniel cleared his throat and Lydia's eyes popped. "Are you going to see Annie?!"

"Why are you yelling, Lydie?" Amy complained. Jacob pulled the buggy away from the Yoder house with a smile on his face as Lydia turned to stare in disbelief at her brother.

"It's about time you took notice of her, Danny Yoder!" she told him. "How long has this been going on?!"

"It's not going on…not really," Daniel mumbled, his cheeks pinkening under his sister's scrutiny.

"Don't you fib at me!"

As the siblings bantered over Daniel's newfound romance, Jacob's chest tightened with happiness.

*This is really it. This is what's supposed to be.*

"Are you two *cooma* to the community center too?" Daniel asked.

"*Nee*, we're going to Rosie's Diner for *nachtesse*," Lydia told him. "But maybe we'll have to stop by afterward and check on the two of you."

"Milkshakes!" Amy cawed.

"*Yah*, milkshakes first," Lydia agreed, smiling affectionately at Amy.

The buggy pulled into Calico, trotting toward the community center, but as they passed the market, Jacob and Lydia gasped in unison.

"Oh..." Lydia muttered. "Is that...?"

"*Wat's* wrong?" Daniel asked as Jacob swallowed thickly, unsure of what to do as his eyes fell on the obnoxious, oversized truck.

"He's still here," Jacob mumbled, more to himself than Lydia.

"Who?" Daniel pressed. As the buggy rolled past, the door to the truck opened and Billy jumped out, the passenger side opening at the same time. On impulse, Jacob stopped the cart.

"Oh, Jake, no!" Lydia whispered, looking nervously at Amy.

"Stay here," he ordered, dismounting the buggy.

"Where is he going?" Daniel demanded.

Billy hadn't seen him yet, but as he neared, his mother-in-law glanced over her shoulder, the blood draining from her face. "Jake!"

Hearing his name, Billy whirled around. An ugly smile formed on his lips. "Oh, look! The weird Jesus freak emerges from his hole."

Anger surged through Jacob, but he managed to keep his composure. "Don't be rude, Billy. You're a guest in this town."

Clarissa looked around desperately as Jacob neared the pair. "You shouldn't be here. Your presence is disruptive."

"We're minding our own business," Billy barked back. "You're the one bugging me on a public street."

"Billy, whatever you hope to achieve by being here, it won't bring Nancy back," Jacob told him calmly. Clarissa mewled at the mention of her late daughter. "I lost my wife, too. Amy lost her mother. Let's not make this any more difficult than it already has been on everyone."

"You don't tell me how to handle the loss of my sister when you're the one to blame!" Billy exploded, racing to cover the distance between them, his face directly in Jacob's. Suddenly, Daniel was at Jacob's side, his face flushed and furious.

"Get away from him!" Daniel cried. Billy barely stepped back to look over the smaller but irate young man.

"What are you going to do about it?" Billy taunted. Through his peripheral vision, Jacob saw Daniel's fists ball and panic overtook him.

*Oh no, Danny!*

Abruptly, Daniel was pulled back and Simeon stood at Jacob's side, several other men making a wall between the simmering young man and Billy.

"Look at this Amish army!" Billy chortled, rubbing his hands together. "I've never seen such a bunch of freaks in one place."

Jacob struggled with his breaths, every one painful against Billy's insults. Clarissa's eyes darted around as if she was seeking an escape.

"Billy, you're disrupting a peaceful town," Jacob told him evenly. "You aren't welcome here."

Billy shoved him and Jacob toppled back, falling into the crowd of onlookers behind him.

"Jake!" Lydia gasped, but he straightened himself and returned to his place, looking Billy in the eye.

Billy leered. "What's the matter, Jakey boy? You forgot how to throw a punch since you entered this bible-thumping cult town? Come on, hit me. You know you want to."

"I'm not you, Billy. I don't solve my problems with violence," Jacob replied evenly, although his insides were quivering. He desperately wanted to knock the smirk off his brother-in-law's face, as he had in the past, but from somewhere inside him, a higher power had forbidden it.

Again, Billy pushed him and again, Jacob stood up, the wall of Amish men growing thicker around him. Not one raised their hands toward him, their bodies simply forming around Billy as his stance grew more uncertain.

"Billy!" Clarissa choked. "Let's...come on."

"Give us Amy!"

Jacob shook his head. "No judge is going to grant you custody of Amy when you're attacking non-violent men in the street, Billy," he offered reasonably. He nodded toward a group of English teenagers, their cell phones recording every moment of the altercation. "This is going to be on TikTok in five minutes."

Billy's face drained of color and he started to shake his head, his attention turning toward the kids. "Give me your phones!" he yelled, but the wall around him was impenetrable. No one was allowing him to go anywhere, least of all near the children.

"BILLY!" Clarissa shrieked. "Get in the truck! We're leaving! NOW!"

With a final, hateful glare at Jacob, Billy whirled around to follow his mother, who had already climbed back into the passenger side, her body quivering with the effort.

Honking wildly, Billy pulled out of the spot and zoomed out of his space, narrowly missing hitting some of the onlookers.

"What a psycho!" one of the kids muttered. "Did you get all that on vid?"

"Yep," another replied. "That's going viral, for sure."

Jacob released a breath he hadn't realized he was holding, the exhale so intense it was a gust of wind. He looked to Daniel first, who stood with his father.

"Are you all right?" he asked Lydia's brother.

"I-I...*yah*," Daniel mumbled sheepishly. "He got me so mad..."

"I know," Jacob agreed. "He has that effect on people. But you're okay now. He's gone."

"You didn't get angry though, Jake," Simeon pointed out. "You kept your composure, even when he put his hands on you."

Jacob shrugged and nodded. "It took some restraint, but that's not who I am. I know we can't solve problems with violence. That's not what we do."

Simeon placed a hand on Jacob's shoulder. "You really do understand our ways, don't you?"

Jacob laughed shakily. "I like to think I'm getting there," he replied, his eyes lifting toward Lydia. "I've had a great teacher."

"*Komme*, let's get you back to the *haus*. I think it's time we talked to Bishop Kauffman about your baptism."

Jacob stared at him, dumbfounded. "I-I—do you really think I'm ready?" he asked, warily.

"Do you want to wait?" Simeon asked pleasantly, glancing at his daughter. "Because I suspect I know at least one person who would like to see you baptized so you might announce your intentions to marry… eventually."

"*Daed!*" Lydia choked, aghast. She shook her head vehemently. "I never said anything like that to him—"

"Why not?" Jacob asked gently. "I know that things aren't usually done like this."

He gestured at the mob of people standing around. "But nothing about us has been traditional from the start. *Yah*, I would like to be baptized if Bishop Kauffman will agree to it."

Simeon beamed. "*Gut*, then it's settled."

"Milkshakes?" Amy squeaked, forcing everyone to turn around. Her blonde head poked up from the back of the buggy, and the Yoders and Jacob burst into chuckles.

"All right, peanut," Jacob agreed. "Milkshakes first. Baptism talks afterward."

# EPILOGUE

## EIGHTEEN MONTHS LATER...

Lydia beamed at herself in the glass as Annie brushed her hair, her best friend's smile identical in the mirror.

"I still can't believe this," Annie gushed. "I feel like I'm going to pinch myself and wake up from a dream."

"Don't pinch yourself," Lydia warned, her own mind having gone there herself over the past year and a half. "We have a wedding to attend."

Annie's smile widened, and she smoothed her hand over Lydia's auburn tresses. "There. Now you have to do me."

The women quickly switched seats as someone knocked on the door. Esther Hertzler entered, her bright eyes shining to see her daughter at the vanity table.

"Aren't you ready yet?" she teased. "You've been up here for hours."

"There are two of us, *Mamm*," Annie reminded her. "Two brides mean twice the time."

"I know," Esther agreed. "I'm just so eager to see you married."

Esther paused and peered at Lydia speculatively as the woman brushed at her daughter's hair. "Are you sure you don't mind sharing your wedding day with Annie?"

Annie's mouth parted in the reflection, her eyes growing large.

"*Mamm*, I'm sitting right here!" she complained as Lydia laughed.

"Annie and I discussed it and there is no one I would rather share my special day with than the *frau* who has always been like a *schweschder* to me…and who is marrying my *bruder*. It seems perfect, doesn't it, Esther?"

Esther smiled and nodded. "As long as you didn't get convinced to do it. I know how Annie can be."

"*Mamm!*" Annie complained, and Esther held up her hands.

"Okay, I'm going."

"Can you find Amy?" Lydia suggested. "Last I saw her, she was eying the barn, and I warned her not to get all dirty but she's three so…"

She offered Esther a sheepish look.

"I'll check on the *maedel*, but I think her *vadder* had her last I saw," Esther replied. "I'll make sure she doesn't soil her dress —at least until after the ceremony."

"*Denki*, Esther."

Annie's mother left Lydia's bedroom, and she resumed her friend's hair, but the blonde stopped her.

"Did I force my way into your wedding?" she asked worriedly. "I didn't think—"

"*Nee!*" Lydia told her firmly. "Your *mudder* is wrong. You and I discussed this at length and if I didn't want you at my side, marrying Daniel at the same time, I would have said so. It seems so right that we would get married at the same time since everything began at the same time. Don't doubt this for a second."

Annie smiled weakly and Lydia gave her an impulsive hug. "You really will be my *schweschder* after today. *Gott* heard all of my prayers and made them so."

Annie sniffed and nodded, her lovely eyes glistening. "Mine too," she admitted. "I never thought I'd see the day when your *bruder* would acknowledge me."

"Daniel is slow, but he's not totally *schtupid*. That's comforting to know," Lydia joked. She pivoted Annie's shoulder back toward the mirror. "Now, let me finish your hair before both Jake and Danny think we've changed our mind about them."

"Wouldn't that serve them right?" Annie giggled.

"Maybe," Lydia agreed. "But what would we do about Amy?"

～

The entire district had come out for this wedding, the combination of both pairings making for the event of the fall and crowding the Yoder property like never before.

"I don't even think we've hosted this many people at worship," Simeon commented absently.

"Isn't everyone supposed to come to worship?" Jacob commented, wiping his hands nervously on his pants. He didn't know what was taking Lydia and Annie so long, but he could see that Daniel was growing antsy too as they waited.

"*Yah*, but look how many *Englischers* have come out, too."

Jacob hadn't noticed before, but as he gazed around the mob of well-wishers, he realized that Simeon was right. Among the community were several townsfolk that knew either Annie, Daniel, or Lydia.

*But not us.*

A pang of sadness crept into his soul at the realization that he and Amy had no family of their own supporting this union.

*At least Oscar lived long enough to know that I was baptized and the Amy and I were allowed back into the community,* he thought, thinking of his recently passed grandfather. *He got to reconnect with Gideon Kauffman a couple of times before he died.*

As if reading his thoughts, Simeon placed a firm hand on his shoulder.

"We are your *familye* now, Jake. And we will be for the rest of your lives."

Gratefully, Jacob raised his head and smiled at his future father-in-law, weighing the difference between him and Clarissa Winston in his mind. But before he could thank Simeon for all he had done, he caught sight of Amy's skirt hem disappearing into the barn and he groaned aloud.

"I'll be right back," he promised, jutting out after his mischievous daughter.

"Oh no you don't," he called as she tripped after one of the wayward hens. "Get back here, Amy."

Guiltily, his child froze in her tracks, her body pivoting slowly as she stared at him with wide, innocent eyes.

"I wasn't doing anything," she fibbed. "The chicken—"

"Is where she's supposed to be. Are you?"

"The wedding hasn't started yet!" Amy complained. "I was just—"

"Amy," he interjected, scooping her up into his arms. "You know, you promised *Mamm* that you wouldn't chase after the animals today."

"I'm not getting dirty!"

"Not yet, you're not, but if you keep going after them, you're bound to get filthy. Come on, peanut. The wedding is about to start."

"Everyone keeps saying that!" Amy protested as he marched them both out of the barn. "But it's been…"

She trailed off as they exited, Lydia appearing with Annie at her side from the side door of the house.

"I told you," Jacob whispered, dropping Amy gently to her feet as her eyes bugged with excitement.

"Is it really happening, Daddy?" she whispered, happiness lacing her words. "Are you really marrying *Mamm*?"

Jacob nodded, suddenly unable to find his voice as his eyes locked on Lydia's, her gaze finding his face.

Amy danced between them, squeaking like a mouse, unsure of what to do with herself until Esther came to collect her and steered her out of the way.

Daniel found his bride and the two couples found their places before the Bishop and ministers, who had been patiently waiting for the ceremony to start.

"Hi," Jacob whispered.

"*Hallo*," Lydia murmured back.

"Are you ready for this?"

Lydia beamed. "I've been ready for this since the day I met you, Jacob Troyer," she replied.

"Shh!" Annie hissed, and they pursed their lips together with a grin.

"Let us begin with a prayer," Bishop Kauffman proposed, and Jacob hung his head, already knowing what his would read in his own mind.

*Our prayers are answered. Denki, Gott, for keeping us safe and protected.*

~*~*~

**I do hope that you enjoyed reading my story.**

**May I suggest that you might also like to read my 'Amish Love and Faith Collection' - 24 Book Box Set that readers are loving!**

**Available on Amazon for just $0.99 or Free with Kindle Unlimited simply by clicking on the link below.**

**Click here to get your copy of 'Amish Love and Faith Collection - 24 Book Box Set' - Today!**

## Sample of Chapter One

Cora giggled and pinned Linda's tresses up higher, the blonde curls falling haphazardly over the younger girl's face. The feeling of the *Englischer* touching her hair was slightly unnerving but Linda didn't pull away. She was slowly learning to tolerate the brash girl, although with much less gusto than her other Amish friends.

"What about this?" her new friend asked, laughing. "Is this how they wear their hair in Amish country?"

Linda swatted the brunette away playfully, her blue eyes alight with laughter. It was moderately amusing how little the *Englisch* knew about their way of life.

"I already told you that we wear our hair in braids most of the time, underneath our caps," Linda replied, turning back to look at herself in the mirror. "You ask so many questions about my home. It's not all that exciting."

"Please!" Cora laughed. "It's not every day I get to meet a real-life pack of Amish kids. You bet your ass I'm going to ask all the questions I want."

Linda flushed at Cora's free speech, the color tinging her cheeks well enough for the other girl to notice.

"And look at you! Turning red just because I cussed!" Cora howled. "How are you guys still in existence in this day and age?"

Cora guffawed as something occurred to her.

"Oh, they are going to love you tonight!"

Linda blinked and looked at the girl curiously.

"Tonight?" she echoed. "What's tonight?"

Cora glanced toward the hallway where the voices of the others could be heard talking and laughing in the living room. Leah was always the loudest, demanding that the channel be changed on the television. Linda wished Cora would go back out there with the others and let her read in peace.

"Didn't Mark tell you? We're going to a party tonight," Cora explained. Linda shifted uncomfortably in her seat, maintaining her wan smile but the thought made her nervous.

*Is there ever a night when some kind of social event isn't happening?*

It wasn't that Linda was opposed to gatherings. She simply did not like the way the English passed their time.

"What kind of party?" she asked. Cora shrugged and flopped onto the bed.

"It's just a bunch of kids from school. Drake's dad's out of town and he always has huge bashes when he can. It's gonna be wild! You'll have a great time."

"Oh."

Uncertainly, Linda met Cora's gaze in the mirror.

"Oh what?" Cora demanded, sounding annoyed.

"I-I don't know..." Linda continued slowly. Cora grunted.

"The others are right about you," she complained, her voice rising an octave as she folded her arms over her ample bosom. "You are boring."

Linda's smile faded away, a twinge of hurt shooting through her. She knew she shouldn't care what the others thought about her because she didn't want to drink, smoke cigarettes or whatever was in that foul-smelling burning paper they passed around. Being Amish was not a popularity contest but during *rumspringa*, Linda was learning that all the rules from home were out the window and she couldn't deny that the words hurt.

"Who said that I'm boring?" she wondered before she could stop herself. Cora shrugged again.

"I don't know. Someone said they couldn't believe you'd even come to Philly for your… what's it called again?"

"Rumspringa?"

"Right," Cora went on. "They thought you wouldn't be brave enough to do the trip."

Every word Cora spoke drove another needle of upset into Linda's heart. It was true that she had not wanted to take the trip into the city but her mother had been worried about Linda's cousin, Leah.

"You must go and keep an eye on her, *lieb*," Hannah Schwartz begged her youngest daughter. "Leah's judgement is not as good as yours. You being there will keep her from forgetting where she comes from."

"But *Mamm*, the point of *rumspringa* is for her to find herself," Linda had complained. In the end, Hannah had appealed to Linda's guilt and there she was on a trip she could have done without.

"Anyway, I'm not surprised that you're bailing," Cora went on, jumping up from the bed. "Your cousin said you probably wouldn't want to come. I guess it'll just be more fun for us while you sit around here being boring."

Linda chewed on the insides of her cheeks as she pondered on Cora's words.

*I don't want to go to a party with a bunch of Englisch drinking and swearing,* she thought. *But I did come here to watch over Leah. If something happens to her and I'm not there...*

She shuddered to think about it.

"*Nee*, I'm coming," she said as Cora ambled toward the door. The brunette paused, a slow smile creeping over her face.

"Yeah?" she asked. Linda forced a beam and nodded quickly.

"*Yah*, for sure."

Cora squealed and clapped her hands, rushing to give Linda an unsolicited hug, again making her tense.

"You're going to have so much fun," Cora promised, turning back to rifle through Linda's trunk that was already open on the bed. "Let's see if you have anything suitable to wear. Drake is going to love you! I told him all about you guys and he really likes blondes."

She winked meaningfully at Linda who turned her head away before Cora could see her blush again.

*That's just what I need,* Linda thought dryly. *A romance with an Englischer.*

But she did not speak her thoughts aloud. In two days they would be returning to the district where she could resume her quiet life without four roommates and their incessant desire to corrupt themselves in every possible way. In another month, she would be baptized and then the only interaction she would have with English teenagers would be when she was at the market.

*It will be fun,* Linda told herself as she studied her face in the glass as Cora continued to chatter behind her. *When will I ever get another opportunity to attend an event like this?*

Yet, even then, she could not suppress the inexplicable feeling of dread rising in her gut, as if God was trying to warn her away from whatever the night held.

**Click here to get your copy of 'Amish Love and Faith Collection - 24 Book Box Set' - Today!**

# A NOTE FROM THE AUTHOR

**Dear Reader,**

I do hope that you enjoyed reading '**For the Sake of His Beloved Daughter**'

Possibly you even identify with the characters in some small way. Many of us presume to know God's will for our lives, and don't realize that His timing often does not match our own.

The foremost reason that I love writing about the Amish is that their lifestyle is diametrically opposed to the Western norm. The simplicity and purity evident there is so vastly refreshing that the story lines derived from them are suitable for everyone.

Be sure to keep an eye out for the next book which is coming soon.

**Emma Cartwright**

∼

**Thank You!**

Thank you for purchasing this book. We hope that you have enjoyed reading it.

If you enjoyed reading this book **please may you consider leaving a review** — it really would help greatly to get the word out!

∽

**Newsletter**

If you love reading sweet, clean, Amish Romance stories why not join Emma Cartwright's newsletter and receive advance notification of new releases and more!

**Simply sign up here: http://eepurl.com/dgw2I5**

And get your *FREE* copy of **Amish Unexpected Love**

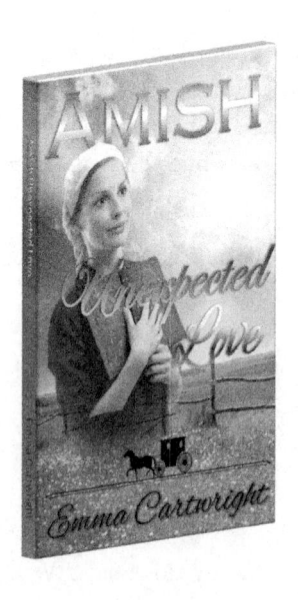

∽

**Contact Me**

If you'd simply like to drop us a line you can contact us at **emma@emmacartwrightauthor.com**

You can also connect with me on my new **Facebook page.**

I will always let you know about new releases on my Facebook page, so it is worth liking that if you get the chance.

**LIKE EMMA'S FB PAGE HERE**

I welcome your thoughts and would love to hear from you!

I will then also be able to let you know about new books coming out along with Amazon special deals etc

Printed in Great Britain
by Amazon